F-

Boy

By Nia Rich

Facebook: Author Nia Rich

Cover: Tina Louise

Editor: Venitia Crawford

Chapter 1

You couldn't have told me that Wes was a fuck boy when I met him. He was fine as hell, and I was smitten the moment that he spoke to me. I was standing in the living room of my friend's house talking with my cousin Nikita. My friend Bianca, who is also a stylist at my shop, was having a house party/ barbeque at her house.

It was the beginning of summer and everyone was feeling summertime fine in their fresh new outfits and hair do's. I know that I was looking fly and feeling sexy. I was showing off my summertime body that I had worked on all winter. My cousin and I spotted Wes when he walked in the door. He was muscular and chocolate just like I like them. Bianca had a song by the rapper Future blasting through her indoor and outdoor speakers. Nikita and I had our red plastic cups filled with some mixture that Bianca had in a glass beverage dispenser on the table. I didn't know what was in it, but it had me feeling right.

"Who is that?" My cousin asked me.

"I don't know, but he is fine." I said to her as I watched him work his way through the crowded house. He slapped hands with a few people and continued through the house to the backyard.

"He is here, so he must know Bianca." Nikita said.

"Right. I wonder if he is one of her guys." I said.

"Naw, I have never seen him before."

"Well, he need to be one of mine." I said. Nikita laughed and took a sip of her drink.

He wasn't wearing a suit, but he had his grown man sexy going on. There is something about gold rimmed sun glasses on a man that is very attractive to me. Bianca and I decided to go out back to mix and mingle and hopefully get another look at him and his friend. We didn't know that they were standing in the kitchen. We were a little embarrassed when we stepped into the kitchen and saw him and his friend standing by the sink. We played it cool and walked past them. He smiled at us and said, "Hello."

We spoke back and kept it moving. We started giggling when we got outside. A fine ass man will have a woman giggling with her bestie at any age.

"Girl I'ma need him to not be that fine!" Nikita said.

"I know girl. Do you think I should go and talk to him?"

"No girl that will make you look desperate. If he likes you he will talk to you."

"Right. True, but he did already speak." I said. I took a sip of my drink.

"Girl stop." Nikita laughed. I laughed with her.

I'm the type of woman who isn't scared to go after what I want, but I am certainly not the type to look desperate while doing it. We stood there and bounced to a Drake song while we were watching people arrive. A few of Bianca's other girlfriends were there. They were ratchet as hell. I saw a couple of thots walking through the back yard in booty shorts that looked like they couldn't breathe in them. Nikita and I were shaking our heads. Then, a couple cuter men walked into the party, but none of them were as attractive as the guy that was standing in the kitchen.

Bianca walked up to us and asked, "Are y'all having a good time? Do you need anything?" Bianca is short, thick, and has a lot of booty. She is always wearing something skin tight that shows off her curves. She is brown skin with shoulder length hair. She never wears a weave. She likes to keep her natural hair relaxed and straightened.

"We good, but who is that cutie in the kitchen though? Is that you?" Nikita asked her. Nikita and I have always been thick as thieves since we were kids. Nikita is tall, brown skin, and hood. She isn't skinny by far. Nikita is top and bottom heavy, and she never lost her stomach after having her son. She likes her weaves short, her nails long, and she always has different colored contacts in. That day her eyes were hazel.

"Who?" Bianca asked.

"The one with the shades on." Nikita said.

"Who Wes? I don't know him. I think that he knows my brother."

"Oh alright."

"Why? You tryna holla?" Bianca asked.

Nikita laughed and said, "Nah I was just being nosey."

I was glad that she didn't throw me under the bus. The last thing I wanted was for Bianca to go in there and tell him that I was interested. She is a live wire like that. I do not like to look desperate. I would rather go in there to speak for myself.

"I need to get some more drink." Nikita said. Bianca's party was a daytime event. It was only three o'clock in the afternoon, and Nikita was already past her limit. I knew that it was only a matter of time for her to start acting ratchet.

"Alright." I said.

"I'll go with y'all. I want to introduce you to my auntie. She is hilarious." Bianca said. Nikita and I followed Bianca back into the house.

Wes was standing up against the wall in the kitchen with his friend. They were drinking out of red plastic cups. He had taken his sunglasses off, and I could see him eye balling me when we walked in. I was the last person to walk in, and he was looking only at me. I acted like I didn't see him, but he spoke to me anyway.

"Excuse me, Ms. Lady. Can I talk to you for a second?" he said to me as he touched my hand. Nikita and I turned towards him. She smiled and said, "Go ahead girl. I will be right back." She followed Bianca back into the living room.

"What is your name beautiful?" he asked me.

"My name is Adara." I said.

"Nice to meet you Ms. Adara. My name is Wesley, but people call me Wes for short."

"Nice to meet you as well Wes." I said.

"This is my cousin Quinten." he said.

I said, "Hi."

Quentin spoke to me, then he turned to Wes and said, "I'll be back cuz." He walked towards the living room.

"So, what is something as gorgeous as you doing here?" Wes asked as he took my hand into his. I blushed and said, "My cousin and I were invited by the lady of the house."

Wes said, "Well, I am glad that you came."

"What are you doing here?" I asked.

"My boy invited me."

"Where are you from?" I asked Wes.

"I am from Philly." he responded.

"I can tell by your accent."

"Yea?" he smiled.

"Yes. How long have you been here in Minnesota?"

"Almost a year. I guess my accent hasn't left me yet huh?"

"No, it hasn't."

He laughed and said, "Dang is it that bad?"

"Nah, it's cute."

"Cute huh? Well, thank you Ms. Lady."

"Why did you move here?" I asked him.

"For work."

"What do you do?"

"Construction." I wasn't impressed with what he did for work, but he had a job which is more than I can say for most of the guys I had been running into. When I met Wes, I was on this kick about only dating a professional man, but I had dated many professional men and I wasn't getting anywhere. I was feeling Wes, so I gave it a chance. It was time for me to try something new.

"What do you do? If you don't mind me asking."

"I don't mind. I am a salon owner." I said.

"Do you do hair also? Or do you just own the business?"

"Yes, I do hair as well. I have been in the business for ten years. My salon has been open for three years."

"That is amazing. You're beautiful, talented, and smart." He nodded his head with a look of admiration on his face.

"Thank you." I smiled and sipped my drink.

He looked at his phone and said, "I am sorry to interrupt this wonderful conversation and leave so abruptly, but I have to go and take care of something. I would love to continue this conversation with you over coffee sometime, if that is alright with you?"

"Sure." I said.

"What is your number?" he asked.

As he put my phone number into his IPhone 7, I looked at his well-manicured nails, clean shaven face, and perfect hair lining. Wes was too sexy and I was already feeling him too much.

"When is the best time to call you?" He looked in to my eyes. I liked the way his dark brown eyes twinkled under the kitchen lights. He was giving me full attention which was a plus. I don't know how many times I had been talking to some guy and I would see his eyes wander to the next chick that was walking past. Wes was not paying attention to anyone else but me.

"Anytime is fine." I said.

"Alright Adara, I will be talking to you soon. It was nice meeting you." he said and rubbed my chin. I felt butterflies when he touched me.

"Ok. It was nice to meet you too." I said to him.

His cousin Quinten came back into the kitchen and asked, "Are you ready?"

"Yea." Wes said and followed Quinten out of the back door.

"Girl he was too fine." Nikita said walking up with another red plastic cup of drink.

"Wasn't he?" I smiled.

"Yes girl! Do you think he gonna call?"

"I hope he does, but if he doesn't, I am not going to trip. He probably got a lot of women anyways."

"Maybe not. Not every fine one is a hoe."

"Yea, but your man is."

"Giiirl for real and I am about ready to cut his ass if another bitch calls my phone."

"See what I am saying? So was Donte and I thought because he was a ball player it would be different."

"I don't know how you thought that when we live in the times of "Love and Basketball" and "WAGS" reality television shows. That should be enough to tell you that these professional athletes are hoes just like a regular guy.

They are even worse because they have money and access to many women." Nikita said.

"True, but that is television. A lot of that is made up for ratings. I thought Donte was going to be true to me." I said.

"Well you thought wrong." She said and took a gulp of the drink in her red plastic cup.

Donte is my ex-boyfriend, or my ex Fuck-boy as I like to call him. He is a professional athlete that couldn't keep his dick in his pants. After baby number two with another woman, I was done with him. Five years of my life wasted on his no-good ass. I kept justifying the things he was doing because he gave me everything I wanted. The money, the house, the jewels, even the car that I am driving now. But there ain't enough money or material things in this world that could have made me keep putting up with his fuck-boy bullshit. I gave back his credit card, kept everything else, and left. Thank God I was already purchasing my house before the breakup and my car was in my name.

My life picked up a lot after breaking up with Donte. I put my focus on my career, and opened my salon. I dated a little bit, but I wasn't interested in anyone; until I met Wes. After meeting Wes, I was totally optimistic about love again.

Chapter 2

It had been a couple of weeks since I met Wes at the party, and I had only communicated with him through text messages. I decided to play the "I'm busy" game for a little bit just to see if he would keep trying and he did. The day that we went for the first date I decided to talk to him on the phone. I was at the gym getting in an intense workout. I was trying to burn off the carbs from the night before. Nikita and I had gone out to a concert and had pizza afterwards. Between the many drinks that I had and the pizza I was sure that I did some damage to my body. I had put in too much work to get my body where I wanted it to let myself go.

Wes called me while I was on the treadmill finishing up a five-mile run. I was listening to Pandora from my phone through my ear phones. I was watching some celebrity gossip show on one of the flat screen T.V.'s in the gym. They were talking about some rapper named Illi-J. I pressed the red stop button on the machine to stop the belt from moving. I used the white towel that I had draped over the top of the machine to pat dry my forehead, face, and neck. I saw the call come through as I was wiping down the machine, but I ignored it. Then I got a text message.

Hey Miss Lady. How are you?

I text back before starting my leg work out.

I am good. How are you?

I am great, but I would be even better if I get to see you again, or at least hear your voice. I know that you are busy, but can't a brotha get a call?

I laughed when I read that text message. It had been half a month since I'd met him. I could have waited longer, but I was eager to talk to him as well. I called him when I finished my workout.

"Dang you are a busy woman." He said when he answered the phone. His sexy voice was like music to my ears.

"Yes, I am a bit of a work-a-holic." Which was true. I love being at my shop making money. That is how I pay my bills.

"I hope that you make time for yourself beautiful woman."

"I do."

"Do you think that you could make some time for me?"

"Maybe." I smiled.

"Maybe? That's cold."

I laughed and said, "I am just kidding."

"So, what are you doing today?" he asked.

"I just finished working out."

"Are you free to grab some coffee with me? No pressure, but I would really like to see you again."

I wanted to see him again, so I agreed to meet up with him. I went straight home to shower and get dressed. I called my cousin while I was flat ironing my hair.

"Girl guess who I am meeting up with today?"

"That cutie from the party? What was his name, Wes?"

"Yes girl. I am doing my hair right now."

"What are you going to wear?"

"I don't know. Probably just something simple like some shorts and a cute top. I mean we are only going for coffee. Who goes for coffee on a first date anyway?" I laughed.

"I know. I was going to say the same thing."

"Especially on a Sunday afternoon."

"At least he is taking you some where though. I don't remember the last time my baby daddy has taken me anywhere."

"I will call you when I get back so I can fill you in."

"Ok."

I had to hang up with her quick, I wasn't in the mood to hear about her trifling man Jakari. His cheating ass is no good for anyone. Nikita's man is a pretty boy barber who has slept with almost every pretty stylist who has stepped foot in the salon he works for and some clients too. Jakari is a shop hoe.

He is light skinned with light brown hair and grey eyes. His eyes always get women going and he knows it. Jakari thinks that he is God's gift to every woman. He knows that he is fine and because of that he treats my cousin Nikita like shit. He talks down to her. Sometimes I want to beat Jakari's ass for the stuff that Nikita tells me. I don't know why she continues to deal with his shit. She can do better in my opinion, but you can't tell a chick anything about her man.

After he gave her chlamydia the first time, she should have been done with him, but she took him back. Then, he gave her gonorrhea, and I don't know how many times she has been to the doctor for a bacterial infection. He was probably fucking bitches in the ass and not washing his dick off afterwards. His hoe ass didn't care about my cousin's health at all. He barely cared about his own while he was out there sleeping with different chicks.

On top of that, I couldn't even count the many times he had called her a bitch, a fat bitch, a black bitch, bald headed bitch, or a dumb bitch, and she took him back. After he called her a bitch the first time, I told her to leave. Nikita didn't leave. She made up some excuse why she took him back again. Then, he popped up with a child younger than the one that she had with him. All I could do was shake my head. That would have been the end of it for me.

That was the main reason why I left Donte alone. He never verbally abused me, but he kept popping up with new kids. I figured that my cousin must have liked the bullshit and drama because she stayed with her Jakari. A man can't be verbally abusive, cheating, bringing home diseases, and new kids. That is a conflict of interest in my opinion, but you can't tell Nikita nothing. Six years into their relationship and I still can't stand Jakari's whack ass. Nikita is still holding on to that fuck-boy. I wish that she knew that she can do better.

I finished straightening my long, jet-black, hair. I put on a pair of jean shorts, a blouse, and a pair of wedge sandals. I looked at myself one more time in my full-length mirror. I was looking good and my butt was looking right in my jean shorts. My lifestyle change had done my body some good. I left my house in Brooklyn Park and headed to the coffee shop in Uptown on the south side of Minneapolis.

Wes was already there when I arrived. He had on a nice short set and some fresh white sneakers. He stood up and greeted me with a hug and a kiss on the cheek. He smelled amazing; just like he did at the party. He pulled my chair out for me to sit down and waited until he knew I was comfortable before he went back to his side of the table to sit down.

"You look beautiful." he said as he sat down.

"Thank you and you look very nice." I said.

"Thank you. It is good to finally see you."

"Thank you. It is good to see you too." We ordered coffee. I got a Latte and he got black coffee one sugar and one cream.

"Ewe you like your coffee strong." I said when our drinks arrived.

"Yes, I do." He smiled at me.

"Not working at the shop today?" Wes asked.

"No, we are closed Sunday's and Monday's." I said.

I love my shop. Being a salon owner is something that I am proud of. Doing hair was my only career option because it was the only thing that I was interested in. My mother and my auntie were licensed hair stylists. Since I was a little girl, I was being taught to become one too. I started doing Nikita's hair in middle school. By time I was in high school, I had a full clientele of girls getting their hair done by me and some of their family members too. I started taking cosmetology classes while I was in my senior year of high school. I got my license shortly after I graduated from high school. Seven years later, I opened my own salon and it's doing well. My mom had always dreamed of having her own salon, but she never got a chance to, so she was beyond proud of me when I opened mine.

"So, what do you have going on for your day off?" Wes asked.

"It is my day to relax. I go to the gym and then I rest. I run most of my errands on Mondays."

"So, that means I can have you all day?" he asked.

I laughed and said, "I wouldn't say all that."

"Alright, I jumped the gun a little bit, but I had to try." he said with a big smile.

"I would say so."

"Have you ever been to the art museum?"

"Not since I was a kid."

"Would you like to go?"

"When?"

"Now." he said.

"Um. Sure." I can't lie. I was thrown off by him wanting to go to the art museum. It was not your typical date. Most of the dates I have been were always dinner and a movie types. His choice made me wonder was he just stepping out of the box, or was it something else.

Wes paid for our coffee and I followed him out of the small coffee shop.

"Leave your car here and ride with me. I will bring you back."

"Are you sure? I mean I can just follow you."

"I am sure. You are safe with me, and your car will be safe here."

We went to the art museum, to lunch, and then to an upscale bar for drinks. I was with him all day. I wasn't expecting to be with him all day, but I wasn't mad about it because I had an amazing time with Wes. He dropped me off at my car after the date as he promised. He offered to follow me home, but I told him that I was alright. When I made it home, I called Nikita right away. Nikita answered the phone on the first ring.

"How was it?" she asked.

"Dang cousin!" I laughed.

"What!? I've been waiting all day for this phone call."

"It was great! We ended up going to the art museum, out to lunch, and out for drinks after that."

"Wow, that sounds so romantic girl."

"I was thinking all kinds of negative things when he first asked me to go, but once we went I was amazed at how much fun I had with him. The art museum was wonderful because it allowed us to talk without the pressure of sitting across the table from each other. By time we went out to lunch, I was already feeling extremely comfortable with him. When the date was over, I wasn't ready to go."

"Aww that's good girl! What was he like?" Nikita asked.

"He was a gentleman and he was sweet. He has this sex appeal about him that is hell of attractive. I kissed him on the first date though girl." I said as I stood in my bathroom mirror. I took my blouse off and hung it on the door knob. I picked up my hair brush and began brushing my hair into a wrap.

"So! You are so old school. People kiss on the first date these days. What are you tripping on?"

"My mom always taught me never to kiss on the first date. It makes you look easy." I said. I tied my satin scarf around my wrapped hair. I pulled out one of my Mac make-up remover wipes and rubbed it in circular motions on my face.

"Girl please. That was back in yo' mama's days."

"There is nothing wrong with waiting. That doesn't make me old school. That makes me a lady." I said as I brushed my teeth.

"Anyways, can he kiss?"

"Yes girl, he's a panty dropper." I said with a mouth full of toothpaste.

"Ha -Ha! I am happy for you. I got to go because Jakari just got home. I will talk to you tomorrow."

"Alright."

I hung up, took a bath, and crawled in bed. He called to make sure that I made it home safe. We talked on the phone for a little bit before I turned into sleep. That night, I closed my eyes with a smile on my face.

Chapter 3

After the first date, Wes and I talked every day. We started spending more time with each other. He always sent me sweet and thoughtful texts during the day. When I had time to talk while at the shop, I would call him. I received a beautiful bouquet of flowers at my shop a few days after the first date, and a couple more times after that. All my stylists wanted to know who sent me flowers and had me glowing. I wouldn't tell them.

Wes was generous. He was always offering to help, or pay for things. He was always buying me things especially if he was out shopping. He would send me pics of things that he saw to see if I liked it so that he could buy it for me. He took me out a lot, he was spoiling me to death, and I was enjoying it. He was treating me like a Queen. During a conversation over dinner one night he told that he was only focused on him before he met me, but meeting me changed how he felt about dating. *"I wasn't dating because I was focused on me, but now that I have met you, I am focused on you."*

At first, I didn't believe him, but over time he seemed to prove that he was telling the truth. His phone was never ringing off the hook. He was never on his phone. He never flipped his phone upside down or kept it on silent. He made me feel like I was the only women in his life. I felt special and important to Wes. We went out to eat a lot. He took me to see movies and attended concerts. He made me laugh and I felt comfortable around him. He was always sweet and thoughtful. I enjoyed him.

***

Several dates later, Wes and I went to a Mike Epps comedy show. I wasn't expecting to have sex with Wes that night, but I did. My plan was to wait ninety days and it had only been a little over a month. Of course, things didn't go per my plan. Up until that night, we had never spent the night with each other. We would always go our separate ways after a date. I learned that a few too many drinks can change my decision making. That is how a simple good-bye kiss landed us in my bedroom.

That first time he took his shirt off in front of me, I was in awe of how chiseled his body was. I knew that he was muscular, but I wasn't expecting all that ebony sexiness to be climbing on top of me. He had all sorts of ink tattooed into his skin; mostly on his chest and back. I've always loved how finely crafted tattoos look on a muscular man.

He had this thug style of making love. He was handling me. His manhood was thick and long and he was pounding into me aggressively. He pushed my legs towards the headboard and damn near made me scream. I grabbed sheets, I grabbed pillows, and I grabbed the headboard. He had me moving backwards to get away from him because I couldn't handle him.

"Stop running. Com'ere" He whispered in my ear.

"Shit." I moaned. "I can't take it." I whispered back to him. I grabbed the sheets and moved back a little.

"You can take it baby. Com'ere." He whispered.

He pulled me back to him and pinned my legs above his shoulders.

"Uhhh." I moaned loudly as I felt the thickness of his girth plunge deeper. He gave me short, deep, thrusts until I was accepting it, then, he spread my legs wide and gave me longer more aggressive thrusts.

"Um hum." He moaned. He had me where I couldn't move, he was giving my kitty-kat a thorough punishing.

"Shit Wes!" I screamed out when he hit my spot again.

"Um hum." He moaned. Wes stayed on that spot. He hit it until he felt my walls tighten around him. He knew I was about to have an orgasm, so he didn't let up.

"Your bout to cum?" He asked.

"Yes."

"Yea?"

"Yes." I moaned. I felt my orgasm and I moaned, "I'm coming." I dug my nails into his back.

Wes stopped for a moment to let me feel the orgasm. He watched my body shake and shiver, then, he took one of my breasts into his mouth and began sucking on my nipple. I moaned as the sensation made my body shiver more. He stopped sucking my nipple so he could kiss me. As we tasted each other's tongue's, he grinded into my wetness in slow circles.

"Mmm." I moaned. His lips felt as soft as pillows.

He pulled out of me and flipped me over onto my stomach. He pulled my hips up to him and entered me from the back. He began giving aggressive thrusts again as he pulled my hips to him. I griped my sheets and screamed into one of my pillows. He smacked my ass a couple of time while he was pumping in out of me. Then, just when I thought I was going to tap out, he reached peak. His orgasm was crippling. He leaned forward and couldn't move for a few seconds. He pulled out of me and collapsed next to me. I slowly laid down on my side. I scooted over to him and put my head on his chest. He wrapped one of his arms around me and we passed out.

***

The next morning, I was exhausted. I woke up to Wes making me breakfast. I slowly rose out of bed feeling like I had a hangover. My head was spinning, my legs felt weak, and my kitty kat was sore. I didn't know that he was going to put it on me the way he did. Nothing could have prepared me for the thug loving that he put on me that night. My body felt like I had the most intense workout known to man. *Damn he put it on me.* I thought as I brushed my teeth and washed my face. I put my cotton robe, tip-toed past the kitchen, and stepped outside of my house to call my Nikita.

"I messed up girl." I said as soon as she answered the phone.

"What?"

"I had sex with Wes."

"So."

"So?"

"Yes. Who cares? Your grown and he is grown."

"Yea but I have only been dating him for like a month."

"Girl please with your ninety-day rule. Nobody waits ninety days anymore that shit is whack."

"I do!"

"Girl anyways, so, how was it? Was it good?"

"Way too damn good."

"Is it big?"

"Hell yes!"

"Aw shit!"

"Girl I am over here spent."

"Ha! Where is he now?"

"Making me breakfast."

"Ha! It must have been more than good! You got him making you breakfast 'n shit!"

"I can't with you right now. I am about to go. It's about to start raining out here anyways."

"Bye girl."

I went back inside and sat down at my table to eat the breakfast that Wes made for me.

"Good morning." he said.

"Good morning." I responded.

"Are you ok?" he said. He walked over to me and set a plate of food in front of me. He kissed me and sat down.

"I am a little sore, but I feel great." I said.

"Did you enjoy yourself?" he looked at me with a sexy grin on his face.

I smiled flirtatiously and said, "Yes."

"I did too." he smiled.

I took a couple of bites of the food he cooked. It wasn't bad. He'd made some breakfast potatoes, pancakes, and eggs.

"Your even beautiful without your make-up." He said to me.

I smiled and him and said, "Thank you."

I felt his hand slide up my thigh. The look in his eyes told me that he wanted me again. I wanted him too. I scooted my chair back and stood up. I walked over to Wes and untied my robe. I stood in front of him. He opened my robe, looked at my nude body, and kissed my stomach. I began rubbing his hardened manhood through his boxers. I leaned down and kissed him. I pulled a condom out of my robe pocket and handed it to him. He took the gold package, used his teeth to open it, and slid the latex on. I mounted him and bounce slowly on his pole. He held on to my hips and thrust up into me. He didn't take his eyes off mine the whole time. We stayed like that until I got mine. Then, he picked me up and carried me into my bedroom. He proceeded to lay the pipe until he got his. We were in bed the rest of that day making love repeatedly. That night, he told me that he had fallen in love with me. I told him that I felt the same. That was the beginning. Before it got real.

Chapter 4

By the time the holidays arrived, we were in a full-blown relationship. I remember when he asked me to move into my place with me. He was already at my house every day. He told me that he had been staying at his cousins since he moved to Minnesota so he could stack his money to move into his own place. He said that he was ready to move into his own, but felt that it would be more cost effective if he moved with me. He was already at my house ninety-five percent of the time. He offered to go half on everything with me. I was already handling everything on my own, but I felt like a little extra wouldn't hurt. Plus, I was enjoying having him around all the time. Having him around permanently seemed to be the next step, so I gave him a key and helped him move his things from his cousin's house to mine.

We were so happy and in love that we decided to introduce each other to our families. We chose to do it for the holidays. We spent Thanksgiving with my family. My mother always cooks a huge Thanksgiving dinner, and invites all my family over. She asked me to bring Wes so she could meet him. She said that she wanted to meet the man that I had been spending so much time with.

My mother and older brother liked Wes and welcomed him into our family with open arms. My mother was excited that I had gotten into another relationship after being single for three years. She is such an optimist when it comes to relationships, but she can't keep a man to save her life. My mother had just divorced her fourth husband. You would think that she would be through with men forever, but she was not. She was already dating again. My mother told me that she was not going to let nothing and no one hold her back from the love she deserves. If the right man came along she would try her hand in marriage again. My brother and I thought that she was crazy for even thinking about marriage again.

"I really like him. He is handsome and very respectful. He made me feel old when he addressed me as ma'am, but I appreciated it." My mom said to me. She was standing next to me in the kitchen. I was making Wes a plate of food. I smiled at her. My mom still thinks that she's young and popping and you can't tell her that she isn't. Her body is out of this world for her age. I get my fitness motivation from her. She lost a lot of weight after her last marriage ended. I think she lost over a hundred pounds. She was back to wearing my clothes. Every time she would visit my house, she would be in my closet trying to borrow something.

"I am glad that you like him." I said.

"Do you think he is the one?" she asked.

"I feel like he could be." I smiled at her. She hugged me around my shoulders.

"Good because I am ready for some grandbabies" she giggled.

"Ok but you're jumping too far ahead mom." I said.

"Well, I'm just saying." She laughed and helped me add turkey and stuffing to Wes's plate. I walked back into the living room where he was chit chatting with my older brother. I handed him his plate. I was glowing and I knew that everybody could see it.

"Hey baby sis! I like this brotha right here." My brother said as he stood up and clapped hands with Wes and then headed to the kitchen to fix a plate of food.

Thanksgiving at my mom's is not traditional where as we sit around a table and eat together. Everyone says grace together to bless the food, then, we get food and sit where ever we want in the house. After I made my plate, I sat down next to Wes in the living room to eat. Nikita was sitting on the love seat across from us next to Jakari and their son. She was cheesing in at us.

"Y'all look so cute together." she said to us.

"Thank you." Wes and I said in unison. That seemed to be the theme for the night. Everyone telling us how good we looked together. We soaked up the love. We took a couple of selfies together and with other family members. Thanksgiving was a success, so his family was next on the agenda.

A month later we were flying out to Pennsylvania to spend time with his family for Christmas. I was excited to meet his family and see his hometown. I was even happier to be taking a trip with my handsome man. We were all over each other at the airport and on the plane holding hands and smiling. Strangers were smiling at us. An older gentleman stopped to tell Wes that he was a lucky man, and that we looked good together. I had heard that so many times, I was starting to believe it. Wes fit me like a glove, and I fit him just the same. We were perfect.

That happy feeling was short lived as I got glimpse into the true Wes while we were in Pennsylvania. It was mild, but it should have been a red flag that I paid attention to. The Christmas trip I will never forget because it was when I began to look at Wes differently and question my judgement a little. It was also a trip that I will never forget because it was the trip that I should have recognized the signs and walked away, but I didn't.

Wesley's family was beautiful. They greeted me with open arms the same way that my family did to him. I could see where he got his skin complexion and handsomeness when I met his father. His mother is a gorgeous, light skinned, full-figured woman. I was sure that she had it going on in her day. Her hair was straightened and hanging past her shoulders. She seemed poised, intelligent, and classy. His two older sisters were pretty, brown skinned women, and his brother looked like his twin. They were only one year a part in age. I thought about how excited Nikita was going to be when she found out that he had a fine ass brother.

His mother's house was amazing. It was huge and she had it beautifully decorated with Christmas lights and trimming. Before seeing her Christmas tree, I had never seen one more gorgeous. His mom fell in love with me right away. I fell in love with her too. I was happy to meet them.

Although I was smiling on the outside, on the inside I was frustrated and not able to soak in the whole experience like I wanted to. I was pissed because right before we made it there, Wes snapped at me for causing us to get lost while we were driving to his mom's house from the hotel.

I had the address pulled up on the GPS app on my phone because his phone battery had died. I accidentally told him to take a right instead of a left and we got lost. He had gotten very angry as we were trying to find our way back to the right highway.

"I am sorry bae. I didn't mean to get us lost."

"Well if you would have known what you were fucking doing, we wouldn't be fucking lost!" he yelled at me.

I was taken aback by his anger towards me. He was too angry for something that little. I had never seen him mad and he had never yelled at me up until that day. His certain burst of anger made me nervous. I just looked at him and kept my mouth closed. I couldn't believe that he had yelled and cursed at me like that. The way he was glaring at the road as we pulled into a gas station made me feel uneasy. He had this crazy look in his eyes.

As soon as he came to a stop at a gas pump, I got out of the car and walked towards the store. *This dude is tripping.* I thought. I felt disrespected. I walked into the store just to calm down. I had no intensions on buying anything. I just didn't want to be anywhere near him at that moment. I took a few deep breaths while standing by the coolers looking at all the different beverages in the coolers. I was acting like I was looking for something to drink. Wes came storming into the gas station looking for me.

"What's up Adara?" Wes asked me aggressively as he approached me by the coolers. I guess I was in there too long. My stomach started to turn.

"Nothing. I just wanted to get some water."

"Well get it and let's go. I figured out how to get there." he said.

I opened the cooler, took a bottle of water out, and handed it to him. He took the water from me, paid for it and the gas, and walked back to the car. I was silent the rest of the ride to his mother's house. I was so frustrated when we pulled up and it was showing all over my face.

"I am sorry that I snapped at you. I was just frustrated that we got lost." Wes said.

"Yea, but that doesn't give you the permission to yell and curse at me. I was just trying to help you."

"I know bae. You're right and I apologize."

"Ok." I said, but my face was still frowned.

"I know you're mad at me right now, but can you at least put a smile on your face before we walk in here? I don't want you to meet my family looking like you want to kill somebody."

Although I was ready to pack up and fly back home, I put on a happy face for his family.

"How have you been?" His mother asked him. We were sitting around the family room after dinner. We were all talking. They were getting to know me and catching up with Wes.

"I have been good mom." Wes responded.

"It's so good to see you son. How is-"

Wes cut her off by shaking his head. "Everything is good mom. It's good to see you too."

I noticed that he cut his mom off, but I never questioned. His mom changed the subject and began asking me questions about my line of work. Seemed like Wes was having too much of a good time drinking and talking with his brother Terence. By time the night was over, Wes and his brother Terence had gone through a whole bottle of Hennessey. Wes was so drunk that he could barely walk a straight line. I had to drive us back to the hotel in a city that I knew nothing about. I did not know that Wes could drink like that. The Wesley that he showed me back home was too humble to get sloppy drunk. I soon learned that his humble nature was all just an act. What I saw in Pennsylvania was the true him.

After he gave me some drunk sex, he passed out next to me. I was so irritated. I sat up and watched a marathon of a reality show about choreographers. A girl named Chelice is my favorite character. "What the hell did I sign up for?" I asked myself. Little did I know that was only the tip of the iceberg.

Chapter 5

Things were as they should be when we returned to Minnesota after leaving Philadelphia. New Years was a blast. We celebrated with Nikita and Jakari, Quinten and his girl Nataya, and my girl Bianca and her boo Troy. Let's just say, we were not the couple acting a fool that night. Nikita and Jakari got into a huge heated argument. They were going at each other's throats outside of the club. We had to pull them apart. Wes and I laughed about it for weeks.

I fell completely in love with Wes on Valentine's Day. I was no longer thinking about the Christmas fiasco. Wes sent me on a scavenger hunt through my house. He had flowers, candy, a beautiful dress, a pair of designer heels, and my favorite perfume set up at the house. Once I was dressed, he had a limo pick me up and bring me to meet him at a restaurant Downtown Minneapolis for a candle lit dinner. After dinner, Wes took me to a romantic Hotel where he had the floor and the bed decorated with rose petals. He couldn't have been more romantic. We made love that night and passed out together. I woke up to the sound of his phone buzzing sometime after midnight.

Who the hell could be calling this late? I thought. I picked up his phone to stop it from ringing, but then I noticed a text message, so I read it.

I guess you're with her.

"What the hell?" I whispered. I took his phone, tip-toed into the bathroom and called the number back.

"Who is this?" I asked when the chick answered the phone.

"This is Kat. Who is this?" she asked.

"This is Adara Wes's girlfriend."

"Oh, well where is Wes?"

"He is sleep. It is after midnight. Who are you? and what do you need?"

"So, I guess Wes didn't tell you about me?" she said.

"Tell me what?"

"I am his wife and we have two children. He forgot to tell you that huh?"

"Excuse me?"

"Yea. I guess you were the reason why he didn't come to visit us while he was here for Christmas. I am sure he is passed out drunk, right?" I thought about it. She was right. He did drink a bit much that night, but I was drinking too so I wasn't paying too much attention to it. I decided not to give her the power of knowing.

"He is sleep."

"Yea well when he wakes up, tell him to call me. His kids want to see their father, and if he tries to lie about me and the kids, you can call me back, or have him call me back while you are there."

"How long have you been married?" I asked.

"Long enough, but I'll let him tell you that since I see that he is still a liar." She hung up on me. I looked at the phone. *I know this bitch didn't just hang up on me. I should call her back.* I thought. I decided not to call her back. I wanted some answers from Wes. I stormed out of the bathroom and back into the room. I picked up a pillow and whopped him upside the head with it.

"Wake up!" I yelled. I whopped him upside his head again. "Wake up Wes! I yelled again.

Wes jerked awake. "What did you do that for? What is your problem?"

"You're married!?"

He sat up slow and wiped his eyes. "Where did you hear that?"

"From the horse's mouth!" I showed him his phone.

"Give me my phone bae."

"No! Not until you tell me if it's true!"

"You have kids and a wife!?" I said standing over him.

"Adara sit down so we can talk."

"No! Answer my question!"

Wes rubbed his eyes again. He was trying to wake all the way up and grasp everything that I was saying.

"I have been wanting to talk to you about that. I just haven't had the chance."

"You haven't had the chance in eight months?"

"Things were moving so fast between us and I couldn't find the right time Adara."

"So, you *are* married?"

He took a deep breath and said, "Yes, but we are separated."

I dropped his phone on top of the blanket and I walked away from him. I began to get dressed. He got out of bed and tried to talk me out of leaving, but I wasn't hearing it. I opened my overnight bag and pulled out my clothes that were supposed to be for the next day. I put my jeans on over my pajama shorts. I put my coat on over my pajama shirt. Slid my UGG boots on and walked out of the door. *How dare he conveniently forget to tell me that he was married and has children.* I thought. I got into one of the cabs that were parked in front of the hotel and went home.

Chapter 6

It had been a month since I had told Wes to not come back to my house. I had my locks changed and I dropped his things off at his cousin's house. I wasn't trying to hear what he had to say. I was extremely mad that I had to find out about his marriage the way that I did. That information was need to know information that Wes should have told me in the beginning. I blocked him from my phone and all my social media pages. I didn't want any contact with him at all. I had never dealt with a married man, and never planned to deal with one.

One day, Wes showed up at my shop with flowers. Of course, all my stylists were smiling and being nosey. I never told them that we had broken up. I felt irritation when I saw him walk in. I was finishing up my client. After my client paid me, I walked them out, then, I approached him.

"Yes?" I asked. He handed me the flowers. I took them and acted like I was happy because I could feel all eyes on me.

"Can we talk?" he asked.

"Sure, but not here."

"There is a Denny's down the street. We can go there."

"Alright. Give me a second to get my coat."

I walked with the flowers in hand to my office in the back. I put the flowers on my desk. I pulled my blue pea coat on and buttoned it. It had to be about 30 degrees outside, so I also put on a pair of gloves, and I wrapped a scarf around my neck. I followed him out the door and got into the passenger seat of his truck. We drove about a block and half down the street to a Denny's restaurant on the corner.

After we were seated in a booth, we both ordered cups of coffee. It was mid- morning and God only knows that I needed a pick-me-up. He was looking me over, as I was doing the same to him. He was looking good to me, but I was still very upset about Valentine's Day.

"You look beautiful as always." he said.

"Thank you. You look handsome as always."

"Thank you." He leaned back to let the waitress set our hot cups of coffee in front of us. While the both of us added sugar a cream to the coffee Wes said, "I haven't been able to stop thinking about you."

"Is, that, right?" I rolled my eyes.

"A little sarcasm. Ok. I understand." he said.

"Why did you come here Wes?"

"Because I needed to see you and talk to you face to face. I figured that would be the only way that you would listen. I hoped that you would have calmed down by now."

"I am."

"You don't want to be with me anymore for real?"

"No."

"Ouch. You don't mean that."

I crossed my arms in front of me and said, "I do."

"Aight listen. The truth is I am married. My wife and I are now separated and have been for a couple of years. We have two children."

"You didn't think that you should have told me that?"

"I was going to tell you Adara. I was just trying to find the right time. I knew that you weren't going to be happy about it."

"Hell, no I am not happy about it. Your wife shouldn't have had to tell me."

"You're right. I should have told you, but her and I do not have anything going on at all. We haven't since we separated. The only dealings we have is our children and that is it. Period."

"So why not get divorced Wes?"

"Because I haven't had the money."

"But you've had the money to buy a car and buy me things."

"You have a point."

"How old are your children."

"Eight and Five."

I shook my head. It was just a lot.

"I know Adara. It sounds worse that what it is baby. I miss you. Can we figure out a way to get past this please?" I was silent for a little while.

"Adara you're really going to sit here and act like you don't miss me? I know you do so stop acting."

He was right, but that still didn't erase the fact that he is still legally married.

"When will you file for divorce?"

"As soon as I get the money. I promise."

"Any other kids that I should know about."

"Well…. No I am just kidding. I only have those two."

"What are their names?"

"Micah and Taylor"

"Two boys?"

"Yes"

"Anything else that you need to tell me?"

"No. Can I have a kiss now?"

"No."

"Stop playing." He stood up and slid into the booth next to me. "Give me my kiss."

I kissed him. I was trying to be unforgiving, but it wasn't working. I missed him and I wanted him back. He spent the night that night and gave me the best sex I ever had in my life. It was somewhere in between making love and straight fucking. It was fast and slow. It was gentle and aggressive. We missed each other, so we were into each other. We looked each other in the eyes the whole time. There weren't a lot of sounds being made between us except when he found my spot and hit it until I had an orgasm. He did that a few times and I screamed every time. When he busted, he grunted loud. He damn near collapsed on top of me. We both laughed as we tried to catch our breath. We lay next to each other in our sweat and juices on one side of the bed. Both of us were trying to avoid the wet spot that we created.

"I missed you." he said in between breaths.

I missed you too." I responded. I dabbed the sweat on my forehead with the back of my hand.

"Are you sure? I mean you got rid of a brotha like you were taking out the garbage or something."

I laughed. "Stop it. It wasn't that serious."

"Yes, it was. You moved my stuff and changed the locks. Damn."

"Maybe, but you shouldn't have lied to me."

"I know baby and I apologize, but we shouldn't ruin this moment by talking about that again."

I pursed my lips and then I said, "Alright, but you brought it up."

"I am ready to come home bae. I can't stand being away from you this long."

"It's been hard for me too Wes." I started placing kisses on his chest. He was looking so good and tasty like a chocolate bar. Especially with sweat glistening on his muscular body. I felt like I had no control over myself. I couldn't stop kissing him.

He looked at me with his sexy grin on his face and said, "You missed this dick, didn't you?"

"Um hum." I hummed in between kisses. He chuckled.

"Stop kissing me unless you want to get a round two started."

"I do." I said.

"Oh yea?" he asked.

"Um hum." I smiled. That was all I needed to say because he climbed back on top of me and proceeded to give me another session of the best sex that I have ever had. Wes moved back in a week later.

***

As soon as Wes moved back in, he was back to doing stuff around the house. He fixed my closet door, put a screen back in one of my windows, and he mowed my front and back yard lawn. He fixed my sink that had been leaking, and he started building a bookshelf for me. I was cooking for him every night. After we both made it home from work, we would curl up on the couch and watch movies, or one of our favorite television series. We played spades and tonk on rainy days. We had even started walking around the lake when it wasn't too cold outside.

I had been so lost in love with Wes, I hadn't made the time to hang out with my cousin Nikita, so while Wes was at home painting the living room the color I wanted, I slipped out to go on a shopping spree with my cousin so we could catch up.

"Damn bitch I haven't seen or heard from you in weeks!" She said when she got out of her car. We hugged and started walking from the parking ramp into the Mall of America. Spring season was finally around the corner, and it was time to get some new fashion.

"I know girl. I am sorry."

"Um hum, so your boo is back and you're too busy getting some dick to be talking to me huh?"

"Whatever!" I said and pushed her away from me."

"For real. I know how it is girl so I ain't hating"

We walked into the Mall of America and decided to start on the first floor. The Mall of America is so big that you can get lost in it. It can take several hours to walk around the entire mall. I was sure that once we got around the first floor, we would be tired. When I visit the mall alone, I only go to the stores that I like and I leave. Since I was having a girl's day out with my cousin, I was ok with taking our time. We would spend most of the time talking and window shopping anyway.

"Are you happy that he is back at your house."

"I can't lie. I am girl. I missed him."

"What about his wife?"

"He promised me that he will get a divorce."

"Do you believe him? I mean what if he is still messing with her?"

"Well she is all the way in Pennsylvania, so unless he starts taking a bunch of trips I won't feel suspicious. I can only take his word for it. He says that they haven't dealt with each other since they were separated. That was two years, ago."

"Um, so what about the kids?"

"I don't know how I feel about that yet. I mean how do you hide two whole kids? I guess I will see how I feel when I meet them."

"Did he ask you to meet them, or did you want to?"

"I want to meet them. If I am going to be in a relationship with a man who has kids, it's only right to meet them."

"I hear you. So, basically you're going to be a step mom?"

"Oh hell no. I will not be letting any kid call me their step mom unless I have a ring on my finger."

"I hear that girl! I have been with Jakari for six years, but I don't deal with his other kids at all."

As petty as it sounds, I don't think I would want to deal with the kids my man had while still in a relationship with me either. I am a mature woman, but I haven't reached that level of maturity yet. It would take some growing for me to get to that level. I think I would feel angry every time I saw them. I know it's not the kids fault, but I don't think I could handle that. That is the reason why Donte and I could never be; ever again.

"Oh, before I forget. Chanel is coming with us to dinner tonight."

"Her bougie ass."

"She is not bougie."

"Yes, she is. I don't know why you don't see it."

Chanel is my best friend that I have known since I was born. Her mom and my mom went to high school and were best friends. They were pregnant with us at the same time. I guess we were meant to be since conception. We are more like sisters than anything. Since neither one of us have a sister, we appreciate the life long bond that we have.

"When did she get back into town?"

"Yesterday."

"I am sure her ass will have on all designer labels. Watch what I tell you."

"What is wrong with designer labels?" I asked as we walked through a Victoria Secrets store. Both of us had one of their shopping bags on our arms. I picked up a pretty lace bra in my size. "Do you like this girl?" I asked.

"Yes, I like it. They always make cute stuff in your size, my breasts are too big for this store. Does Chanel always have to flaunt? She only as big as a toothpick."

I laughed and said, "You sound like a hater. Come on, she does work for one of the top fashion magazines, so you have to expect her to have the best of the best in fashion."

"I understand, but there is nothing wrong with Rainbow stores and Forever 21."

I laughed. "I can't with you right now. You know damned well if you had it, you would be buying designer labels too. You stay running around here with fake coach bags that you and you baby daddy bought from the purse lady, so shut up."

She laughed and said, "Whatever." We walked out of the store after paying for our things and started walking through the mall again.

She flipped her maroon colored lace front wig off her shoulder.

"I see that lace front that I made for you is holding up. The color still looks good on it."

"Yes, girl I love it. Jakari hates it."

I rolled my eyes. "Why this time?"

"He said it was too long, but I was like whatever. This wig got me feeling all Beyoncé and shit."

I laughed. "That's right. Don't listen to him. That wig looks good on you. I did it, and you know that I wouldn't send you out here looking crazy."

"I know he is just a hater. Girl I went up to his shop yesterday and one of those new stylists kept eyeballing me. I was about to smack the shit out of her, but I heard your voice in my head telling me to be a lady. Plus, I didn't want to mess up my new wig."

I laughed. Her baby daddy was up to no good as usual. I was not surprised to say the least.

"For real girl, I think that she is fucking Jakari and let me find out that she is. I am going to beat that bitch's ass."

"Now what is that going to solve? It wouldn't be the first-time Nikita."

"Nope it won't be first time I beat a bitch ass over Jakari, but it will be the last. I told him that he better not be fucking her or I am done."

I scratched my head. "But you said that the last time cousin."

"I mean it this time."

"Ok."

Nikita knew that she was not leaving that fuck-boy. She knew that she was lying to herself when she said it. I knew that Nikita was lying to herself and me, so I didn't know why she wasted her time saying it. Maybe she was trying to make herself believe the lie. Nikita is my family and I love her, so I didn't challenge her. I would just be there for her when she calls me crying again.

***

Later that night we met up with Chanel at Chino Latino's restaurant in Uptown Minneapolis. It's one of Chanel's favorite restaurants.

"You look cute!" Chanel said to Nikita.

"You look the same." Nikita said back to Chanel.

Nikita made a funny face at me when she hugged her. She was throwing shade. I knew that it was going to be a shade throwing between them the whole time as always. I smiled and stood up to hug my beautiful, brown skin, sister from another mother.

She ignored Nikita's comment and turned to me and said, "I missed you!" She gave me a big hug.

"I missed you too!" I said as I hugged her back. She looked gorgeous as usual. She is a little taller than me, and way skinnier than me. She wears about a size two. The features that always stood out to me about her, is her large forehead that she always keeps covered with bang or a side part in her hair, and her big lips.

Chanel sat down in the empty chair on the other side of the table. "Oh, that is an amazing coach bag you have Nikita. Is it real?"

Nikita rolled her eyes at Chanel. "Yes, it is."

"Oh. It's really nice." Chanel smiled at her and then turned her attention to me.

"So how have things been?" she asked me.

"Girl everything is good." I said.

"You know that I have got to let you get into this hair before I leave." She ran her fingers through her jet-black hair.

"I see that she got up into yours Nikita, nice color."

"Thank you." Nikita said. I was not sure if that was shade that Chanel threw at Nikita, but knowing her, it probably was. She likes to throw shade with a smile and a soft sweet voice. Chanel ordered a bottle of wine when the waitress came to our table. Nikita stopped the waitress before she left the table.

"Excuse me. May I have a Long Island Ice Tea.?" Nikita asked the waitress. The waitress nodded her head, wrote Nikita's request down on a small notepad of paper, and walked away.

"You still drink those?" Chanel asked.

"Yes, I do." Nikita said with attitude.

"I haven't had one of those since college." Chanel said.

"Looks like you haven't found a good dermatologist since college either." Nikita said. She was referencing the little bit of acne that Chanel had on her forehead.

"Looks like you haven't found a good nutritionist darling." Chanel said to Nikita. She was talking about Nikita's fluffy middle section of her body.

"Ok girl." Nikita said.

"Ok girl." Chanel responding in a snobby tone.

They were throwing low blows so I decided to intervene. I rolled my eyes at Nikita before I said, "So what's been up with you?" I asked Chanel.

"Besides meetings, flights, and deadlines I haven't had time for life. I don't even remember the last time that I was on a date or had my edges sweated out."

All three of us laughed.

"What's up with your new boo? I can't wait to meet him."

"He is great. He is at home waiting for me to get there."

"Is he cute?"

"Hell yea." Nikita said.

I scrolled through my phone's photo gallery to find a picture of Wes and me. I reached over and showed her the picture.

"You two look good together."

"Thank you."

"So, what does he do?"

I hesitated, then I said, "Construction work."

"You are with a blue collar brotha? I can't believe you. What would make you do that?" she asked while removing her Michael Kors sunglasses. She put them on the table next to her handbag by the same designer.

I knew that she was going to judge him because of his job. There was a time when her and I only dated business men and athletes. I guess at one time, people used to call them ballers, and call us gold diggers.

"What's wrong with that? He has a job." Nikita said.

"I would expect *you* to say that. He *can't* be making any money. How the hell is he going to do *anything* for you living off pennies."

Nikita rolled her eyes. "Bitch please."

"If you haven't noticed sis, I am doing just fine taking care of myself. Maybe it's not what he can do for me financially. He can do other things."

"Like what? Give you some dick? Shit any man can do that. At least make sure that it is worth it. Money makes it worth it."

"My man does enough for me with his blue-collar money. I guess the latest athlete you're dating is worth getting cheated on and disrespected, right?"

"Whatever. I am sorry, but I don't know about him being the one for you sis."

"Sis, you don't know and I don't know, but right now I am in love, so if you don't mind, I would like to end this conversation. Excuse me."

I stood up to step away from the table for a minute to call Wes back.

"You are a disrespectful bitch." I heard Nikita say as I walked away.

"Hello."

"Hey bae. You have been gone all day."

"I know. I am sorry. Girls day out can get a little long sometimes."

"Hurry up and get your ass here."

"I am."

"When?"

"Soon."

"I got something for you when you get here."

I giggled and said, "You're nasty."

"Um hum and you like it."

I saw Nikita walking up to me to make sure that I was ok.

"I'll be there soon.

"Aight. I will be waiting."

When I got home, Wes was waiting with candles lit and soft music playing. He ran bath water for me, bathed me, gave me a full body oil massage. I thanked him by taking him into my mouth. I kissed the head of his chocolate bar a few times before I wrapped my lips around it and took all of it into my mouth. The look of love in his eyes as I gave him oral pleasure turned me on, and I couldn't wait to climb on top of him and feel his girth inside of me. I sucked on him until I had him on the edge of cuming and moaning my name. Then, I climbed on top and bounced on it until he busted. I must have done the damn thing because he wrapped me up in his muscular arms and passed out. He did not let me go for the rest of the night.

Wes and I went out to dinner with Chanel before she had to leave town. She was all hugs and smiles, but I could tell that she was being fake. She questioned him a lot, and it made him feel uncomfortable, but he smiled through it and took control of the conversation by asking her questions about her. I was impressed by how he handled her. I gave him the best sex ever that night too; to thank him for being such a gentleman with my sister.

"You know that you are stuck with me, right?" he asked after we made love that night.

I giggled and said, "What do you mean?"

"I mean, I ain't going nowhere. We are going to be together forever."

"You want to be with me forever bae?"

"Yes, I do. You are the one for me. I couldn't have found another woman who is more perfect for me than you. I love you."

"I love you too."

We passed out in each other arms again. I was floating in the clouds again, and things were normal. For a little while.

Nia Rich

Chapter 7

"Bae I need you to come and get me."

"From where? What happened?"

"I am down here off Bloomington Avenue and Lake Street. These mutha fucka's are towing my truck."

"What?"

"Yea man. Can you come now please?"

"I am on my way bae." I said.

I was at the salon talking with one of my stylists about bringing a barber into the shop to rent a booth from me. I told her that I would be right back. Wes wasn't too far from the shop.

When I pulled up he was standing on the corner looking pissed off. He got into my Porsche Cayenne truck and slammed the door.

"Stupid ass mutha Fuckas!" He said angrily.

"What happened?" I asked.

"They pulled me over and took my shit!"

"Why bae?"

"Because I was driving with no license and no insurance."

"No license? You've been driving around with no license Wes?"

"Yea and these dicks had to pull me over!"

"I am confused Wes. Why don't you have a license?"

"Because I don't!" His voice was extremely escalated. Wes was pissed off and I was still trying to grasp the fact that he hadn't had a license the whole time that we'd been together. I was trying to wrap my mind around why a grown ass man didn't have a driver's license, and why Wes had never told me.

"Yea Wes but why?"

"Adara don't start with a bunch of questions and shit! I am not in the mood!" he yelled.

There was that temper again. There he was, taking his anger out on me again; just like when we were in Pennsylvania. I knew that me questioning him might have been annoying, but I was just trying to figure out what was going on. I felt that I wasn't doing anything more than any loved one would do.

"I am sorry. I am trying to figure out what is going on. I am just finding out that you have been driving without a license."

"This ain't the time for that shit Adara! Take me home!" he yelled. His voice echoed through my truck.

"Don't yell at me Wesley!" His yelling at me made me angry. It wasn't my fault that his car got towed.

"DON'T SAY SHIT ELSE TO ME! JUST TAKE ME THE FUCK HOME ADARA!!!!" he yelled again. and hit the dash board with his open hand.

I started driving. I was furious. There we were arguing again about something that he did not tell me. *Here is another thing that he conveniently forgot to tell me, and now he is yelling at me again like I did something to him. Just when everything was going good. Here is this drama, and right before our one- year anniversary.* I thought.

We drove in silence. He didn't say anything when he got out of the car. He slammed the door shut and walked away. I shook my head and pulled off. When I returned to the salon I was in a foul mood. I stayed in my office for the rest of the day until closing time.

I didn't say anything to Wes when I got home. It was the first time that I felt like I didn't like him. I was mad at him when we were in Pennsylvania, but this time I wasn't feeling Wes at all. I can understand being angry, but Wes yelling at me like I put him in that situation was not alright.

He was sitting on the couch watching television when I walked in. I rolled my eyes at him when I walked past him. I was giving him the serious silent treatment. I set my purse on the bed, took off my shoes, and walked into the bathroom. I slammed the door and locked it. After I got out of the shower, I put lotion on my body, and slid into my satin robe, I heard Wes wiggle the bathroom door handle.

"Open the door Adara." he said through the wood door.

I ignored his request. I finished wrapping my hair to keep my flat iron style fresh and silky looking. I tied a satin scarf around my wrapped hair and stared at my reflection in the mirror. I heard Wes wiggle the handle again.

"Bae open the door." he said.

I opened the door and walked past him. I walked over to my dresser and pulled out a satin night gown. He followed me and watched me take my robe off and put the night gown on. Then, I walked over to the bed, pulled the covers back, got in, and closed my eyes.

"Bae." He said. I pulled the cover over my face.

"Aight." Wes said and then he walked away. I heard him go back into the living room and sit down on the couch. I laid there until I fell asleep. I woke up to him crawling into the bed next to me. I felt him kiss me a couple of times to wake me up. "I'm sorry." he whispered.

I could feel his hardened manhood up against my butt. He turned me over onto my back and climbed on top of me. I opened my eyes and saw him looking down at me as he pushed himself inside of me. "I love you." he whispered as he slowly pumped in and out of me.

I closed my eyes and let him have me. I felt his soft lips kiss mine and I got lost inside of his sexual pleasure. I opened my eyes and moaned. "I love you too."

All my anger dissipated with every stroke. At that moment, the argument that we had earlier that day was no longer important.

***

I got up the next morning to make breakfast. He walked into the kitchen wearing only his boxer briefs. He hugged me from behind and kissed me on my shoulder.

"Good morning beautiful."

"Good morning." I responded.

"I am sorry that I yelled at you yesterday."

"I know, but it's not ok for you to take your anger out on me Wes."

"I know bae and I apologize."

I turned the stove off and scraped the scrambled eggs from the pan onto the two plates of food that were on the counter next to the stove.

"Are you ready to talk now?" I asked.

"Yes bae."

I turned toward him, adjusted my satin robe, and gave him direct eye contact.

"I don't have a license because I just got off parole when I met you." Wes said. My heart dropped into my stomach. I raised my eyebrows and said, "Parole?" *Please Lord tell me that I am not dating a criminal.* I thought.

"Yes."

"So, you're a criminal?"

"Don't say it like that."

"How am I supposed to say it?"

"I did some time on some drug related charges. That is the past. I am focused now."

"Why didn't you tell me that in the beginning?"

"Because I figured that you wouldn't give me a chance if you knew."

"Wesley." I said disappointedly.

"I know."

"When we had the talk about your wife and kids, I gave you the chance to tell me about anything else that I didn't know. You could have told me then."

He sighed loudly. "Please don't start Adara."

"Please don't start what?"

"Arguing with me."

"Wes I mean-"

"You mean what Adara? I've been off parole for a year now. I am working, I am not in the streets. Please don't make this bigger than what it is."

I pursed my lips because I had more to say.

"Please." he said.

I held my tongue and said, "Fine."

"I love you ok? Let's eat before this food gets cold."

I followed him to the table with our plates in my hands. Seemed like as time went on more and more skeletons started dropping out of his closet. I started to question my judgement of Wes. I started to wonder had I made a mistake getting into a relationship with him. I knew that both situations were small things, but most times small things end up turning into something bigger later. You couldn't have told me that then. I was in love with Wes, so I chose to push forward even though my gut was telling me to walk away.

Chapter 8

Only a woman, who is crazy and in love, would let a man drive her vehicle without a license. Wes was driving around my Porsche Cayenne truck without a license every day, and he had been for months after his car was towed. There were days when he would drop me off at the shop, have my truck all day, and then come and pick me up when I was ready to leave. I hated for him to have my truck sometimes, but I worked with him. I was in love with Wes, so part of me wanted to do what I could to help him. Wes told me that he was going to get another car, but he seemed to be moving slow about doing it.

"I didn't see your truck parked out front. Wes must have your car again." My girl Bianca said when she walked into the salon.

"Yes, he does."

"Seems like he has your car a lot girl. What happened to his car?" *This bitch is being too nosey.* I thought. I loved Bianca but I was sensitive about Wesley's car situation. It was embarrassing, and I didn't want anyone to know.

"It broke down and we are in the process of getting it fixed." I said.

"Oh, ok girl. You a good one for letting him drive your Porsche around." Bianca said as she took her tools out of her bag and laid them out across her station.

"I know." I said. I felt like she took a shot at me on the slick, but I ignored it. I felt that I might have been in my feelings a little bit. I watched her walk over to the receptionist desk to see if she had any appointments in the log. Her booty bounced and jiggled with every step. Sometimes I wondered what it felt like to have an ass as big as hers. I turned my swivel chair towards the mirror at my station and picked my phone up. I sent a text to Wes.

Where are you? You were supposed to be here over thirty minutes ago.

I put my phone back onto my station. I was supposed to be meeting up with Nikita for some girl's time together, but Wes had not shown up and was not responding to my text messages. I tried calling him, but he didn't answer. I text message Nikita to apologize for running late. I didn't know what was going on with Wes, so I told Nikita that I would reschedule with her.

Thirty minutes after I text Wes he called me back. I was sitting in my office fuming. "Where are you?" I said angrily.

"Sorry bae. I got caught up with my cousin."

"I called and texted you Wes."

"I know. I left the phone in the house charging and we were in the garage."

"You couldn't charge it in the garage?"

"Adara I am pulling up now!" he yelled.

I snatched my purse off my desk and walked out of the salon. Bianca was still there finishing up one of her clients.

"Bye girl." I said when I walked past her.

"Bye!" she called after me.

I hopped in my truck and slammed the door. I was so pissed that I was silent. I usually go mute when I get mad. It is the only way I can control my anger and try to calm down.

"Bae-"

I cut him off. "Don't say anything to me Wes."

"Would you listen?"

"Listen to what?"

"I apologize that I am late."

"You being late is one thing, but you not responding to me to let me know that you were going to be late, is what I am most angry about Wes. I called and text you several times and you come giving me some lame ass excuse about your phone being on the charger. You expect me to believe that?"

"Adara believe what you want to believe! I don't have no reason to lie to you!" he yelled. I was sick and tired of him raising his voice in a heated discussion. It was like every time he got angry he had to yell. That time he had no reason to be yelling at me because he was the one in the wrong. I ignored the yelling because something else caught my attention.

"Do I smell alcohol?" I asked Wes. He didn't say anything.

"You're driving my car drunk!" I hollered. He had me yelling which is something that I don't like to do.

"I am not drunk Adara. I just had a few beers with my cousin." *Is he crazy?* I thought. He was driving my Porsche truck under the influence, but it was no big deal to him because it was just beers.

"You shouldn't be drinking anything while driving my car!" I yelled.

"Your car!?"

"Yes, my car! Did you forget Wes!?"

"Aight that's cool. I'll get my car and then I won't have to hear this shit."

"You shouldn't be driving any car under the influence Wesley!"

"Alright mom." he said.

I was done talking to him. I turned my head to look out of the window. That was the only thing I could do to stop myself from physically attacking him. My anger was boiling over, and I had to get in control before I smacked him. I didn't talk to him for the rest of that night.

**

Wes knew that I was mad, and he was on his best behavior for about a week. Then he was late again, and a few more time after that. That's when I started to notice a pattern with Wes and his drinking. He was drinking a lot more than usual and every time he came to pick me up I smelled liquor on his breath. He seemed to continue the trend of being late to pick me up no matter how mad I got, and I kept allowing him to use my car.

Bianca noticed one night that I was still at the shop when she was getting ready to leave. She was usually the last one out. She asked me if I wanted a ride, and my pride made me want to say no, but I accepted the offer. I was praying that he wasn't drinking and driving my car again.

"Where is Wes?" she asked.

"I don't know girl, he said he had something to do after he got off work. He told me that he was on his way, but it has been over an hour." I responded.

"Girl I know that you are pissed right now." Bianca said as we were driving towards my house.

"I am." I said

As we were pulling up to my house, Wes called me. I answered the phone quickly.

"Where are you?" I asked Wes.

"On my way."

"Now? I have been waiting for you, for an hour. I am on my way home."

"How?"

"Bianca is dropping me off. Meet me at home."

"Aight." I could tell by the sound of his voice that he had been drinking, but I didn't want to say too much in front of Bianca. It was freezing outside that night and the roads were slick. It had rained and then snowed earlier that day, so there was black ice everywhere on the roads. Anxiety started filling my body as the possibility of Wes getting into a car accident consumed my mind. *He is going to kill himself and wreck my car.* I thought.

"Do you want me to wait with you girl?" Bianca asked.

"You don't have to." I said. She ended up sparking up a conversation with me about the shop and we ended up sitting in the car for a little while in front of my house. We saw Wes pull around the corner and throw a bottle of beer out of the window of my car. I shook my head back and forth. I wasn't sure if Bianca saw the bottle fly out of the window, but I was embarrassed. He parked my car in my driveway, got out, and walked over to Bianca's car. He came to my window and knocked on it.

I pushed the power window button to roll the window down.

"Sup? You coming in or what?" he asked me. "Hi B." He said to Bianca before I could answer him.

"Hey Wes." she said.

"You coming?" he asked me. His eyes were red and his breath smelled like alcohol. I glared at him angrily for a second and then I said, "Yea."

I thanked Bianca for dropping me off at home and I told her that I would talk to her the next day. I followed Wes into the house.

"Bae." he said as I was hanging up my coat.

"Don't talk to me Wes."

"Adara."

"You are not driving my car anymore."

"Damn it's like that?"

"Yes, it's like that. You were driving my car with an open bottle of liquor in the car. Then to throw it out of the car because you didn't want me to know that it was in there. That is disrespectful."

"It was just beer."

"Beer is alcohol. It is freezing outside. You could have gotten into an accident."

"Whatever. I am not drunk."

"What? Do you hear yourself Wes? You are not driving my car anymore. Period." I put my purse onto the couch and walked towards the bedroom.

"Before you go to bed I wanted to tell you that my divorce is final. I was late because I was celebrating with my cousin." I stopped walking and turned to face him. "Are you serious?"

"Yes. Look." He pulled an envelope with paperwork out of his pocket. I looked at it, and I smiled.

"I am so proud of you!" I exclaimed and hugged him.

I was happy. I hadn't mentioned his divorce since we talked about it at Denny's a while back, but I was thinking about it. I was not ok with being in a relationship with a married man even though I was. I planned to ask him about it, but I hadn't gotten around to it. I was too busy dealing with this new drinking habit Wes had. That news was a total surprise.

"I love you baby. I did this for me and you." He said.

"I love you too bae. I am so happy for you, but you still ain't driving my car anymore."

"Baby stop tripping. I promise I will not be late anymore, and I won't drink and drive your car anymore. I am going to get my own car. I haven't bought one yet because I was trying to get this divorce situated first."

"Um hum and you ain't getting any either."

"Yes I am."

"No, you're not. You're on punishment for making me have to get a ride home with Bianca."

He palmed my ass. "I ain't on no punishment this ass is mine." I giggled.

He picked me up and carried me to the bedroom. I was still mad, but I gave him some. He gave me some oral first. He loved to make my body shiver from a tongue orgasm. Words can't describe the feeling of his soft lips sand tongue on my pearl. He pulled me to him, spread my legs and, and kissed on it. Then, he flicked it with his tongue, and sucked on it gently. I returned the oral pleasure by deep throating and sucking him slow. I always loved to watch his eyes roll into the back of his head when he was about to cum. He stopped me right before he lost it, so he could give it to me. He bent me over so he could hit it from the back. I arched my back perfectly for him and threw it back to him. I knew I had him when he tried to stop me so he could catch himself. I kept throwing it back until he lost it and busted. I gave it to him that night because I had to let him know that this pussy belonged to him, but if he kept fucking up he would lose it.

After that night, Wes was acting right again. I chopped everything up as he was just having a moment. He bought me a few gifts to apologize for his behavior. We were having amazing sex every night. We weren't arguing, and Wes hadn't had an angry outburst. I was dropping him off at work and picking him up. Everything seemed to be on the up and up.

Chapter 9

My birthday rolled around so fast I wasn't ready for it. Seemed like after I turned twenty-five, the years kept flying by. I wasn't excited about getting one year older and one-year closer to thirty years old. I wanted to have a blast with everyone that I love for my birthday. I planned to have dinner and drinks and then go out for drinks and dancing. Somebody should have told me that anything involving drinks and Wes was recipe for disaster.

The day started off beautiful. Wes and I spent the day in bed relaxing and then he took me shopping. I was super excited to see all my friends later that night, so I could show off my new engagement ring. Wesley proposed to me while on a trip to Miami for my birthday over the weekend. I hadn't told anybody and I was bubbling with excitement.

My birthday is in the spring, so I picked out the most incredible, form fitted, lace sheath dress. It fit my body like a glove. As I stood in the floor length mirror looking at my new birthday outfit, Wes came and stood behind me. "You look beautiful baby. I can't wait to make you my wife."

"I can't wait to be your wife." I said and smiled. I lifted my hand to look at my ring. It sparkled under my bedroom lights.

"Are you ready to tell your family and friends?"

"Yes, I can't wait."

"You know that you're really stuck with me now."

I smiled and said, "Why do you keep telling me that I'm stuck with you?"

"Because I ain't going nowhere and you can't get rid of me."

I turned to face him and put my arms around his neck. "I love you."

"I love you more."

I was covered with hugs and kisses when I made the announcement at my dinner. Everyone from the salon was in attendance including my Bianca and my new barber/stylist Deon. Chanel was in town. Nikita and Chanel were at each other's throats as usual Chanel was gawking at my ring, I guess she couldn't believe that Wes bought such a beautiful ring on his salary. The truth is, she was right. Wes didn't purchase the ring by himself. He and I both wanted my ring to make a statement, so I helped him. We went and picked it out together and purchased it together while we were in Miami. Wes purposed to me with it on the beach. It wasn't traditional, but I didn't care. I was in love. I promised Wes that I would never tell anybody that I helped him. Especially not Chanel; the Queen of superficial values.

Nikita told me that she was happy for me too many times. Bianca congratulated me and elected herself the bachelorette party planner. My mom was all smiles, but she left early. She didn't want to go out with us. I was happy that she missed when Wes started drinking too much. I was thanking God.

Before we left the restaurant to head to the club he was finishing his third drink. He was talking louder and more than usual. I saw him stumble a little bit on his way to the bathroom. When the waitress came back to our table, he started to order another drink, but I stopped him by whispering, "Baby let's wait until later ok?" He looked at me and nodded his head in agreement. Shortly after that, Wes started questioning me about Deon. Deon is an extremely attractive man, but he is gay. He is just not a feminine gay man. I don't know if Wes felt threatened by Deon's presence at my party, but his focus seemed to be primarily on him.

"What's up with that dude?" Wes whispered to me as we were paying for our bill at the table.

"Who?" I asked.

"Your boy." He nodded his head towards Deon. I knew that Wes was feeling the liquor because he was talking slower than usual.

"Who Deon?"

"Yea."

"Nothing. Why?"

"He talks too much and you are talking to him too much. Do you like him?"

"Wes stop. No I don't." I said with a frown on my face. I knew then, that Wes had drank way too much. Wes asking me about Deon took me by surprise. He had never questioned me about another man before that night.

"Aight y'all let's go party!" I said. Everyone stood up and headed out of the restaurant and over to the club we decided to go to for the night. Luckily, I thought ahead and rented a hotel room downtown. Wes did not stop drinking. In fact, he drank me under the table on *my* birthday. I spent my birthday evening babysitting Wes. I couldn't even enjoy myself because I was too busy chasing him around the club removing drinks from his hands. I had to keep him out of people's face talking about stuff that they weren't interested in hearing. Wes asked me about Deon a million times and got upset when I hugged Deon goodbye. I hugged everyone goodbye, but Deon was his focus. He said his hands were too close to the small of my back. The night ended with us in a cab and Wes passed out on my shoulder. Once again, I had to assist him to walk into the hotel. I didn't even get birthday sex. My birthday was ruined.

***

He apologized for about a week after that. I was starting to get tired of hearing his apologies, but I accepted it. Shortly after my birthday he decided that it would be a good idea for me to meet his children, but his ex-wife refused to let me meet them without her being present. She wanted to meet the woman that he was going to have her around her kids. We told her that we would come to Pennsylvania, but she was adamant about coming to Minnesota. I figured she wanted to see how Wes and I were living before agreeing to send her kids to visit. Although I wanted to be a bitch about it, the woman in me understood where she was coming from.

Wes flew her and his children into town at the beginning of summer. We met up at a Dave and Busters in Maple Grove, and then she came by our house afterwards for a little while. I suggested picking her up or meeting her closer to her hotel, but she insisted on driving her rental car to meet with us. I am not sure why I was nervous to meet her, but I felt nausea as we were driving to the restaurant. All of that went away when I shook hands with the beautiful, well-educated, woman that he used to be married to. She was tall, had a light brown complexion, short cut hair, and was dressed very nicely. She was very polite. His two boys were very well mannered. They looked like she had done a great job with them while Wes was away.

All three of us got along well. Her and I spent most of the time getting to know each other. She was impressed by me and loved the fact that I own a salon. She is an office manager for a law firm, and was working on her degree in Criminal Justice. I couldn't get over how poised and classy that she was. After lunch, Wes took the boys to go play some of the arcade games scattered around the place. He was so happy to see his boys. I had never seen Wes so happy.

"It's good to see Wesley with a good woman." she said after Wes left the table. It was weird hearing her address Wes by his full name.

"Thank you."

"I want to apologize to you if I came off harsh or disrespectful over the phone that night that we talked. I was just so frustrated. I had been trying to get in touch with him for a while and he was dodging me, so I hope you understand. Hearing that he had been home, but didn't come to see his children was very hurtful and disappointing."

"I completely understand. I was upset because I knew nothing about you or the children. I wished that he would have told me."

"That is Wesley for you. You two seem happy. I love it, but woman to woman, the big dick isn't worth all the problems."

I was taken aback by that statement. I heard someone say it in a movie once, but I wasn't expecting to hear it from her. Sometimes when I think back on that conversation, I wish I would have left him. It was a warning that I didn't listen to. Another red flag that I brushed off my shoulders.

Chapter 10

Winter time had arrived again, and we got hit with a big snow storm. I remember because I shut the shop down early. The news was predicting twenty inches of snow or more. They were urging everyone to get off the roads. The stylists and I headed home. I was surprised to see Wes there when I got there. I figured his job had sent everyone home too. Usually he would call to have me pick him up. I called him when I was leaving the shop, but he didn't answer He was sitting on the couch watching the news on T.V. The news anchor was following the snow storm and giving in the moment updates. I stomped my boots on the floor mat to remove snow, then I took them off and put them on the mat by the door.

"I was just getting ready to call you." he said after I kissed him on the lips. I could taste liquor on his breath, but I didn't say anything. I took off my coat and hung it on the back of the dining room chair. I hung my scarf around the collar of my coat, and I set my purse on top of the table.

"What are you doing home so early? Did your job send you home because of the blizzard? I called you but you didn't answer."

"Did you?" he asked and picked up his phone to look at it. "Aw bae I am sorry. I forgot to take my phone off silent." He showed me the missed call on his phone.

"Oh. It's ok. I was just calling to see if you needed me to pick you up from work."

"Yea, about that baby. I have some bad news."

"What?"

"I got fired today."

"What?" I asked. I stopped walking towards the kitchen, I turned around and looked at him.

"What do mean fired? For what?"

"They said that I was drinking on the job."

"Were you?" I folded my arms across my chest.

"I mean I had a couple of shots before I went in this morning, and a couple at lunch but that isn't much."

I dropped my hands from being folded and put them on my hips. "What do you mean that isn't much? You shouldn't have been drinking at all Wes."

"Adara come on, not right now." I took a deep breath, closed my eyes, and reopened them.

"It seems like this drinking is getting a little out of hand don't you think?" He sighed and put his head down.

"I knew that I was going to have to hear your mouth."

"Damn right you're going to hear my mouth. What the hell were you thinking? That is so irresponsible. You're a grown ass man and you know better than to be drinking on the job." He lifted his head and looked at me.

"Adara, I am already pissed about it. I don't feel like discussing it ok?" he stood up and walked past me to the kitchen.

"Well I feel like talking about it." I said as I watched him walk to the refrigerator.

"Bae don't trip! I am going to get another job aight! Shit!" he said loudly, then, he pulled a beer out of the refrigerator.

"You're going to drink some more!?" I asked angrily.

"Yes. I need something to take the edge off Adara!"

"You already been drinking you don't need nothing else Wes!" He had me yelling again. I was not expecting to hear the bullshit he'd just hit me with. If anything, I was expecting to get home and cuddle up with him during the snow storm. Instead, I was arguing with him about his stupid mistake.

"Adara leave me the fuck alone!" he yelled into my face as he walked past me. I turned and walked to our bedroom and slammed the door so hard the pictures on my wall shook. I was pissed, and what infuriated me more was that I was going to be snowed in with his drunk ass.

Wes slid his drunk ass in bed with me that night. I felt him trying to wake me up to have sex, but I ignored him. He loved to have make-up sex. Sometimes I swore that he liked to piss me off just so we could fight and make-up. I knew that he didn't upset me on purpose that night, but he did some stupid shit, and I wasn't feeling make-up sex at all.

Wes knew that I was up so he said, "Bae I know that you are mad at me right now for doing something stupid. I love you. I will make things right."

I took a deep breath and opened my eyes. He was staring at me with so much sincerity in his eyes. I couldn't help but to soften up. He said, "Can you hold me down until I get another gig? You know I am good for it."

"Ok Wes, but you have to get another job." I said.

"I won't ever do this shit again. I promise. I learned my lesson bae."

I closed my eyes. I felt him kiss my lips. He started kissing my neck, and my breasts. Then, he took one of my nipples into his mouth. I felt my kitty purr. I was giving in and I hated myself for it. He continued down to my navel and then he spread my legs and put his soft lips on my lower lips. He began kissing and flicking his tongue on my clit. Before I knew it, I was trapped inside of his oral pleasure and my anger had been suppressed. I rode his tongue until I burst and then he gave me that good dick until I burst again. Wes would always come to me with an apology, and I would always give in. I swore to myself I wasn't going to allow him to do it that night, but I did. That was the night that I realized how weak I was for Wes.

Chapter 11

After that night, I started helping Wes search for a job. I say help, but really, I was doing all the work while he watched. He asked me to help him, but I realized that what he meant by help, was that he wanted *me* to do it all. I put the resume together. I submitted the resume and applications online. I would spend at least an hour at the shop each day searching for jobs for him and submitting applications.

Several months had gone by and he hadn't gotten any real leads on another job. I was at the shop all day, and Wes would be at home. Every time that I would get home from running my shop all day, he would be sitting in front of the television with a beer in his hand, or he would be at his cousin's house drinking Whenever he spent that day at Quinten's house, I would have to go and pick him up on my way home from the shop. He never thought that I would be tired after running a shop all day. I would be pissed that he would go over there knowing that Quinten would be too drunk to drive him home.

I would walk in the house and nothing would be done around the house. I mean nothing. Dishes would be piled up, laundry piled up, bed not made, bathroom a mess, sidewalk and steps not shoveled, and the trash not taken out. I felt like since he was home every day, he could make sure that the house was cleaned. He wasn't doing anything else. He couldn't say that he was looking for a job because I was doing that for him.

Most of the time I wouldn't say anything, I would just get to cleaning and straightening things as soon as I walked into the house. He would sit down and watch television with a drink in his hand while I was cleaning everything.

The drinking had gotten worse. He had gone from just drinking beers to drinking bottles of Hennessey, smoking weed, and smoking cigarettes every day. I had so much frustration that I would slam stuff around the whole time that I was cleaning.

"The fuck is your problem? Why are you slamming shit around!" he asked angrily one night after he took a couple puffs from the blunt he was smoking.

"I don't understand why you can't clean shit around here! You are here all day and nothing is done!" I yelled from the kitchen. I was boiling that night and I was ready to throw one of the dishes I had in my hand at his head. I was standing at the sink rinsing dishes to put them in the dishwasher.

"I wasn't here Adara!" he yelled back at me.

"You woke up this morning! You know that I am at the shop all day! You expect me to do everything!"

"Man, here you go tripping."

"I'm not! You're not working Wes! You could at least do something around here!"

"Don't you think I know that! You don't have to keep bringing that shit up!" he said and stood up to walk towards me. My mentioning the fact that he did not have a job set him off.

"I am bringing it up because it has been months and you haven't found a job yet! Then you're not doing shit around the house! I'm sick of this shit Wes!"

"You gonna find someone better than me? Like that mutha fucka at the shop!?" He grabbed my elbow. It wasn't aggressive enough to make me feel threatened, but it was enough to make me get pissed off and snatch my arm away from him.

"What are you talking about Wes!? He is gay!"

"Gay my ass! Let me find out that you're messing with that dude!"

"Wes get up out my face!" I yelled at him. He stepped back and walked away.

By the time, I finished doing the dishes, he was passed out on the couch. That is where I left him. He slept on the couch the whole night. When he woke up, I was already at the shop. I didn't have any morning clients, so I was taking care of my shop bills when Wes called me.

"You couldn't wake me up last night or before you left?"

"No."

"Why."

"Honestly, I didn't feel like being bothered with you Wes."

"It's like that Adara?"

"Yes."

"Why?"

"You know why. You are starting to drink too much and you are not doing what you supposed to be doing."

"Adara."

"I got to go."

"Why? You don't want to talk to me?"

"No."

"Why not bae?"

"Because I am irritated with you Wes."

"Aight Adara, but can you do me a favor and send my resume to this company? I will text you the info."

I hung up on him. I sent the email like he asked me to, and I was angry about doing it. I could see that one of the things that I was having a hard time doing with Wes was telling him no. I should have told him to send his own damn email.

When I got home from the shop that night, the house was cleaned from the top to the bottom. Wes did the laundry, he did the dishes, he shoveled the walkway and steps, he laid salt over the ice on the walkway, and he was at home and not drunk. He met me at the door. He opened the door before I had the chance to put the key in the lock. I took a deep breath and smiled when I walked in.

"Oh, my gosh, it looks so good in here." I said. He smiled at me and kissed me on the cheek. He closed the door, locked it, and took my coat.

"Thank you, Wes." I said.

"You're welcome." After he took my coat he stood in front of me and said, "I heard you. I've been fucking up. I've been stressed out about not having a job, and I 've been bugging out a little bit. Forgive me please?"

Part of me did not want to forgive him, and part of me was melting like butter. I kept a straight face. I couldn't let him know that he had me weak.

"I don't know."

"Stop being so hard. You know that you love me." He gave me the sexy puppy dog eyes.

"Um hum. Thank you for cleaning. I do love you, but you aren't off the hook that easy. Just because you cleaned this time, doesn't mean that you don't have to clean again.

"I know bae. I got you. Just relax and sit down." He walked me over to the couch, and turned the television on. He put my boots by the door.

"Come on." He took my hand and helped me get up from the couch. He walked me into the bathroom. "I filled the tub up for you. The water is nice and hot how you like it."

I smiled and said, "Awww thanks bae."

"I am just doing what I am supposed to do. When you're finished, meet me at the table. I cooked dinner."

"You cooked?"

"Yes."

I smiled at him. Wes was trying to get back into my good graces and get some brownie points. He was doing a good job. I took a bath and met him at the table, and he set a plate of delicious looking food in front of me. He sat down at the table with his plate of food in hand.

"I want you to relax tonight bae. I don't like it when you are all stressed out."

I took a bite of food. "Mmm you cooked this?" I asked.

He laughed. "Yes."

"If you know how to do this, why do you let me cook all the time?"

"Because I like your cooking."

"That's not right. You need to cook more often."

"I will bae."

After we ate, we both sat on the couch. Wes sparked up a blunt. He took a couple of pulls from the blunt, he blew the smoke out, and then he passed it to me.

"Uh-uh I don't want that."

"Come on bae. Loosen up and chill with me please."

"Alright. This time."

I took a couple of puffs and choked. After I was done choking I gave it back to him.

"Naw smoke some more." I did, then, I passed it back to him.

We ended up smoking half of the blunt. I was so high that I felt like I was in another world. Wes loved seeing me high and being silly. He kept playing with me to make me laugh uncontrollably. We sat back and watched reruns of the Martin television show. We cracked up laughing for hours until our stomachs hurt. Then, we made love on the couch.

Wes always had a way of pulling me back in. Especially when I was too through with him. I had a great time with him that night, and for several weeks after that, but the good times were short lived again.

Chapter 12

The holidays were horrible. We spent time with my family but we were not able to see his family. I spent a lot of my money buying him stuff, but it wasn't reciprocated. Wes went on a couple of temporary jobs that lasted a few weeks each, but it wasn't enough money to do anything with. He had to use the money he made working the temp jobs to buy his kid's some things for Christmas. Although I understood that his kids came first, I was irritated by the situation. We got into a heated argument on Christmas Eve about him not having a job. We got into a huge fight on New Years that resulted in me getting out of my car and walking a couple of blocks in the cold to get away from him. I paid for our Valentine's Day dinner; that he completely ruined because he got too drunk. My birthday had come and gone. We argued that night too. I slept on the couch that night and would not allow him to touch me.

A few more months had past and we were nearing our two-year anniversary. My patience was wearing thin, and I was growing tired of having to pay for everything. I always paid the bill whenever we went out. The first couple of times I was alright with it, but after a while I started to feel like when was something going to give. I was getting sick of hearing him complaining about not having a job, and then not doing anything about it. He was getting lax with helping around the house again. I swore if he walked in the house one more time and threw his hoodie sweatshirt over the arm of the couch one more time, I was going to pick the sweater up and strangle him with it.

"Stop leaving your clothes on the couch!" I yelled as I snatched his hoodie and jeans off the arm of the couch. I tossed it into the hamper in the bedroom.

"Aight bae." Wes slurred. He was drunk again. He'd been hanging out at his cousin Quinten's house as usual. His cousin drinks a lot and he also likes to drink lean and pop pills. Every time Wes came home either drunk or off that lean he would be stumbling around, slurring his words, and talking crazy to me. When he came home rolling off a pill, he would want to have sex with me all night and then once the pill wore off he would be sleep all day. What scared me was how he couldn't remember most of the stuff he did the day after.

I rolled my eyes at him and walked into the kitchen to get a bottle of water out of the refrigerator. "Here you need to drink this." I said while placing the bottle of water in front of him.

"Com'ere." he grabbed my arm.

"No. Don't touch me."

"You don't love me anymore." he slurred. He said that so many times when he was under the influence of lean and liquor. I was tired of hearing it. I rolled my eyes and walked over to the dining room table to get my purse.

"You love the dude at the shop." he said as he watched me walk into the bedroom. It had become a habit for him to bring Deon up every time he was under the influence. I ignored him. I wasn't feeling the bullshit that night. I needed to get away from him. He had been stressing me out so much that I noticed my hair was starting to fall out. I was never happy or smiling like I used to be.

By that time, Wes had been unemployed for six months which may seem like a small amount of time for some, but it is a lot of time when you are the one who is financially responsible for everything, and supporting someone else's habits. I was paying all the bills by myself and taking care of both of us while supporting his liquor, weed, and cigarette habits. He was costing me about fifty dollars a day. Multiply that by seven, then, multiply that by four and you got a car note and rent going into his body for mental stimulation. I was so stressed that I even started smoking cigarettes.

I called Nikita. "Sup girl?"

"Sup witchu?"

"I need a drink and some girls time."

"Girl me too."

"Meet me downtown at Seven Sushi Lounge. Text me when you are leaving out."

"Ok."

I hung up with her and turned my laptop on. I reserved a room at the W hotel downtown Minneapolis. I packed some clothes in one of my big purses. I wasn't planning to come back home. I needed a break from him and the drunk shit that he was on.

"Where are, you going?" he asked when he saw me walking towards the door with my purses in hand.

"I'm going out."

"Going out where?"

"Going out with my cousin." He got angry and quickly stood up.

"Nah, you tryna go meet the dude from the shop?"

"I am starting to see that you are severely insecure Wes! Quit bringing him up! He is Gay! I already told you that once!"

"He ain't gay. He wants my woman." I ignored him and picked my keys up off the table.

"You ain't going nowhere." he said and grabbed my arm.

"Stop!" I yelled and snatched away from him and turned to walk towards the door. He stepped in front of me. "Move!" I yelled and side stepped him.

"Nah! You not going nowhere!" he grabbed my arm again.

I pulled away from him again and yelled, "Stop grabbing me Wes! You're drunk!"

"Nah fuck you mean you bout to leave! I said you ain't going no fucking where!" he followed me to the door and stood in front of it.

"Move Wesley."

"No Adara! Go back to the room because you are not leaving here!"

"Move!" I yelled.

"I said no! Quit fucking playing with me! You ain't about to leave this house and try to cheat on me! You got me fucked up Adara!"

"Cheat on you with who Wes!? I am leaving because I am sick of your shit!"

"I ain't trying to hear that shit!" he snapped in my face. He picked me up and started carrying me through the house. Both of my purses dropped on the floor as I was kicking and screaming. "I hate you Wes!"

"I don't give a fuck. You're my woman." he slammed me on to the bed and laid on top of to hold me down. I was still squirming, but I couldn't break free.

"Stop moving you ain't going nowhere." he said and leaned down to kiss me. I moved my face and he kissed my cheek. We both were breathing hard. I could smell the stench of alcohol on his breath. Had I still been going to the gym regularly like I used to, I might have been able to get him off me. He had all his weight on me causing me to stop fighting because I had run out of breath and energy.

"Call your cousin and tell her that you are not coming."

"No because I am going."

"Fuck with me if you want to."

"I don't have my phone."

"I'll call her from my phone."

He took his phone out of his basketball shorts pocket and called Nikita.

"Yo cousin, Adara ain't coming tonight." I could hear Nikita say, "Alright." He hung up.

"I can't stand you." I said.

"I love you." He tried to kiss me again, but I moved my face.

"I don't want a kiss."

"Shut up. Yes, you do."

"You're drunk Wes."

"Shut up. You're mine. This pussy is mine. You ain't going nowhere ever, and you're gonna have my baby."

Chapter 13

Wes was right. I didn't go anywhere. I paid for our Anniversary dinner a few weeks later. Wes hadn't stopped drinking, and I was sitting up in my shop in the early stages of my pregnancy a couple of months later. I was stressing out about it because Wes was not working yet and I was sure that he was back to selling drugs with Quinten.

My shop was going through some changes and I needed to hire some new stylists. Business had slowed down some and without some good stylists in there that could pay the booth rent, my money was going to be funny. I wasn't getting anything done because I couldn't stop throwing up everything. My favorite season had finally arrived and I wasn't enjoying it. Summertime was not the time for all the madness I had going on in my life.

I was supposed to be driving Wes to his job interview, but I was too sick to do it. I let him drop me off at the shop and take my truck to the interview. He was coming back to get me after the interview. I wasn't going to make it a full day at the shop. I needed to go home and lay down. I fit my cousin Nikita's hair appointment in while I waited for him to come back. I promised her that I would shampoo and style her hair that day. Nikita and Jakari were taking their son to take family pictures at the mall.

I heard her come into the shop. Nikita and Bianca were always so loud when they saw each other. I could hear them cackling from my office.

"Hey Girl!" Nikita said.

"Hey boo!" Bianca said. I heard them both laugh. I figured that they gave each other a hug like they always do.

I didn't feel like getting up from my office chair, so I let Nikita meet back there. I was feeling, sick, tired, and stressed. I was praying that Wes would get hired.

"Hey cousin!" Nikita said when she walked into my office.

"Hey!" I tried to sound upbeat. I am sure that I didn't do a good job it.

"You look tired." she said.

"I know. I do girl because I am." She was right. I usually had my makeup done to perfection, and my hair was always flawless. That day, I was wearing my hair in a ponytail and I was bare faced.

"Do you need me to reschedule?"

"No cousin I can handle doing your hair. Come on." She followed me out of my office and back to the front of the salon to the shampoo bowls. I gave her a shampoo and sat her under one of the hooded hair dryers. That gave me some time to drink some water and eat some crackers. I took her back to the shampoo bowls to rinse the conditioner from her hair, then we walked over to my station so I could put wrap lotion in her hair, wrap/set her hair, and put her back underneath the dryer. That time allowed be to sit down and relax for a little while. After, Nikita's hair finished drying, we walked back over to my station so I could style it.

"What are you going to do?" Nikita asked me as I was flat ironing her hair. She didn't know everything, but she knew enough to know that a baby was not what I needed.

"I am going to have it." I said. Nikita gave me a look of concern. I felt what she was feeling. It wasn't time, but I never believed in having abortions. I was kicking myself in the ass at that moment.

"Has he got a job or a car yet?" She asked.

"No. He is at a job interview right now."

"I hope that he gets it."

"Girl me too because I can't do this anymore."

It had been like eight months since Wes had a steady job. I was still handling everything, and I had dipped into my savings. I wasn't trying to do that.

"Do you really think that you should be having a baby?"

"I know what you are saying cousin, but I can't get rid of a baby. My heart won't let me do that."

"Apparently, your heart won't let you get rid of that man either." I punched her in her arm.

"I know you ain't talking! With that fool you been dealing with for over 6 years!"

"Ow cousin!" she laughed.

"Sup y'all!" Bianca said as she walked back into the shop after smoking a cigarette outside. Although I smoked cigarettes at the time, the smell was making me nauseas.

"Hey girl. You smell like an ashtray."

"Shut up. You sound like a pregnant woman." Little did she know, I was pregnant. I hadn't told her and anyone else in the shop yet.

"Whatever. So, I am having a small get together at my house for my birthday. I want you two and your boo thangs to come."

"I'm down! Are you down cousin?" Nikita asked.

"Yes. We'll be there Bianca." I said.

The first thing I thought about is everything going completely wrong at her party. I hated going anywhere with Wes. I thought about going to the party by myself, so I could have a good time. I knew that Wes was not going to let me go to Bianca's party alone, and I was not going to enjoy myself with Wes by my side. I prayed that he wouldn't embarrass me again.

Wes had gotten possessive over the two years that we were together. Anything I did, he had to be right there with me, or he was going to suspect that I was cheating, or trying to cheat. Part of me was praying that Deon didn't show up. Deon's attractiveness triggers insecurity in Wes. I didn't know what it was, but it was annoying as hell. Especially when I, and everyone else in the shop knows that Deon doesn't even like women. I felt that some of Wes's insecurity was the fact that he knew that I could do better than him. He was afraid that I was going to find someone better, and Deon represented the type of man Wes figured I would want to be with.

I finished up with Nikita's flat ironed style. I had her looking red carpet ready, and I was sure that her baby daddy, Jakari, would have something negative to say about it. Although it was her natural hair, cut short the way they both like it. Jakari would still find some way to tear her down.

I got a call from Wes after I finished throwing up for the third time. I was glad because I was ready to go. The crackers and water didn't stay down. I rushed to my phone to answer it. I hoped that he was going to be on time. I needed to lay down and rest. I was extremely tired and all I could think about was sleep.

"Baby don't be mad." Wes said. I knew instantly that it couldn't be good. I automatically got frustrated because I was tired and I wasn't in the mood for his, *"I am going to be late,"* shenanigans.

"What Wes?" I asked with a lot of attitude.

"I got into an accident." Wes said.

"What!? Where are you!?" I asked alarmingly.

"Over North." Anger instantly filled my body. *What the hell is he doing over North Minneapolis?* I thought. The only reason that he would be going over North is to go to Quinten's house, and I knew that Quinten's house meant drinking and drugging. Quinten's house also meant that they would most likely be making drug run's in my car. Wes knows that I am not ok with him selling drugs out of my truck.

"What are you doing over North Wes!? Your interview was in Bloomington!"

"Bae this is not the time for questions. The police are on their way." he said.

"Shit! Alright. I am on my way." I prayed that he didn't have any drugs or liquor in my vehicle. I hung up and walked back to the main area of the shop with my purse in hand.

"Nikita, can you take me over North? Wes just got into an accident in my truck."

"What?" Bianca asked.

"Is it bad?" Nikita asked.

"I don't know."

"I hope that he is ok." Bianca said.

"Thanks Bianca."

"Come on cousin let's go." Nikita said.

"Let me know if you need anything." Bianca said.

***

Nikita and I got over North in no time. Luckily it was the middle of the morning and there wasn't much traffic outside. I damn near cried when I saw my Porsche truck. The whole front end was damaged. Like I said before, a woman must be crazy in love to let her man drive her car with no license. In my case, my unlicensed, unemployed, alcoholic, drug addicted, fiancé, was driving my Porsche Cayenne truck.

The police gave Wes a huge fine for driving without a license. The only thing that saved him from going to jail was that I showed up to claim my vehicle, and that I had insurance on my truck. I swear I wanted to punch Wes in his face as I watched them tow my car away from the wreck scene. Nikita's eyebrows were up the whole time we were standing out there in the middle of Broadway and Lyndale Avenue.

Wes got into the car with Nikita and I so she could give us a ride home. I was concerned with getting home, so I could find out what needed to be done about my car. I was so angry that I forgot to ask Wes how he was feeling. Honestly, I didn't care. I could see that he wasn't dead and he was still breathing. He walked away from the accident without so much as a scratch, meanwhile, my car was beat up and the damage might have been irreparable.

"Are you ok Wes?" Nikita asked him.

"Yea I am good cousin. Thanks for asking since your cousin over here doesn't even care about a brother."

he said from the backseat of Nikita's car. *Fuck your feelings.* Was the first thought in my head, but I didn't say it out loud. I knew that it wouldn't be right to say that. God would never forgive me for being so heartless.

I mustered up the energy to ask, "Are you ok Wes?"

"Nah don't say something now, you didn't care up until your cousin said something." Wes said.

I might have cared a little more if I wasn't already going through hell of shit with him. I may have even cared more if he was injured or something, but he was sitting up in Nikita's car in tact waiting for sympathy, and I just didn't have any in me. I wasn't in the mood for Wes's melodrama.

I gave Nikita a hug when she pulled up in front of our house. I thanked her and told her that I would call her later. I was ready to cry, but I held back my tears.

"Thanks, cuz." Wes said to Nikita when he got out of the car. She said bye to him and pulled off. Nikita was running late for her family photos because of Wes's bullshit. I held my tongue as we were walking into the house. I snapped as soon as we shut the door and locked it.

"What were you thinking!?" I yelled.

"It wasn't my fault! The girl ran a red light and hit me!"

"Why were you over North Minneapolis in the first place!? You were supposed to be going to a job interview and coming back to pick me up from the shop! Not driving around town!"

"I am a grown man! I can drive where I want!"

"Not in my car Wes!"

"Your car!?"

"Yes! My car Wes! Did you forget again!?"

"Here you go again claiming your shit!"

"Because it's mine! It's in my name and I am the one paying for it! Now, I need to come up with more money that I don't have to fix it! Are you gonna pay for it!? No, you're not!"

"You don't know that!"

"I do know that and you know it too! Were you drinking Wes!? Please tell me that you weren't drinking. You weren't drinking, were you?" I was pacing back and forth. My heart was racing, and I felt like my head was going to explode.

"Would you calm down! I wasn't drinking!"

"But you were on your way to go and drink! That is why you were going over North! To go to Quinten's house, and after I've asked you several times to not drink and drive in my car! I am so sick of you! You tore up my shit! What if I messed up your shit Wes!"

"I just told you that it wasn't my fault Adara!"

"The point is, you shouldn't have been over there anyways!"

"I ain't tryna hear this shit!" He hit the wall with his open hand. "I'm fucking tired of hearing your mouth!"

That was it for me. After he hit the wall, I yelled, "Get the fuck out Wes!" I stormed into the bedroom and started pulling his shit out of the dresser drawers and throwing it onto the bed.

"Adara what are you doing!?" he yelled. I had blacked out and didn't care. I just wanted him to get his shit and get out. I was tossing drawers, socks, and t-shirts. Anything that looked like it belonged to him was flying everywhere in our bedroom. After I finished the dresser drawers, I went straight to the closet and started tossing his shit from the closet.

Wes took his cell phone out of his pocket and dialed Quinten's number.

"Aye cuz, you got to come and get me. Adara is tripping. I'll tell you when you get here." I heard him go outside. I finished throwing his stuff everywhere and sat on the floor with my back up against the bed and my knees pulled to my chest. I needed to catch my breath. Ten minutes later, I heard a car pull up and a car door slam. Wes left without taking anything with him.

I was so mad that I fell asleep on the bed full of his clothes, socks, and drawers. I woke up a few hours later and cleaned up the mess I made. I spoke with the insurance company who told me that my car was totaled. I called the rental car company to reserve a car for a few days until I figured out what to do. More money that I had to spend due to Wes. Additional money that I wouldn't have had to spend if I wasn't with Wes. I text messaged Bianca to tell her that everything was ok, and that I wouldn't be at the shop the next day. I had the receptionist reschedule all my appointments. I would be spending the next couple of days trying to handle my car situation thanks to Wes.

He didn't come home that night, but he sent me a text message that said, *Bae I apologize about your car. It wasn't my fault.*

I didn't respond. I cleaned the rest of the house, and ran a steaming hot bubble bath. I grabbed a bottle of wine, a wine glass, my pack of cigarettes, and my ashtray. I slid into the tub and lit my cigarette. I took a puff and blew a large cloud of smoke out. As the spicy taste of the red wine hit my tongue, I leaned back and closed my eyes. I let the words to "Can't Raise a Man" by K Michelle massage my ears from my phone's Pandora account.

Chapter 14

I woke up to Wes calling me the next morning. I threw up twice last night and my head was pounding. I knew that the wine and cigarettes weren't going to agree with me and the baby that had implanted itself in my uterus, but I was so frustrated that I wasn't thinking. I felt horrible. I told myself that I wasn't going to do that again. I rubbed my eyes before answering the phone.

"What?" I said.

"Are you calm now?" Wes asked.

"Yes."

"I missed you last night bae."

"Um hum."

"Bae I'm sorry."

"Um hum."

"You're not going to talk to me?"

"What do you want Wes?"

"Can I come home?"

"Not if you're going to be hitting walls and stuff."

"I'm not bae."

"Are you sure?"

"Adara I promise. Can I come home?"

"Yes."

"I'll be there soon."

I slowly sat up in my bed. I sat there for a few minutes until my eyes adjusted and my body felt willing to let me walk to the bathroom and brush my teeth. After I brushed my teeth, washed my face, and drank a glass of water, I felt a little better.

Wes walked in about an hour later smelling like weed smoke. His eyes were blood shot red. He took his sneakers off at the door and walked over to me. I was sitting on the couch watching television. I wasn't mad anymore. I was more concerned with getting my car situation taken care of. I told myself that accidents happen, so I was going to do what I had to do to fix it, and make sure that it didn't happen again.

"Hey bae." he said before kissing me.

"Your breath stinks." I said.

He laughed and said, "Well you kicked me out with the clothes on my back."

"You left." I smirked.

"You told me to get out and started going crazy."

"I was mad about my car, and I am still a little heated, but I'm not going to hold a grudge.

"I love you, Beautiful woman."

"I love you too."

He squeezed one of my breasts, but I pushed his hand away.

"No make-up sex for you."

"Why?"

"Because you keep messing up."

"You giving me some of my pussy."

"Whatever."

"What's up with the car?"

"It was totaled."

"Damn bae. I promise I'm gonna help you pay for that. How much do you need?"

"I don't know."

"Well here is five hundred. I'll get you the rest later."

"Where did you get this?"

"I hit a lick with Quinten last night."

"You know that I am not cool with you doing stuff like that."

"I know but I'm about to be getting some major money."

"Illegally."

"It's money."

"It's not ok."

"Whatever."

"It's not whatever. Are you trying to go back to prison? How are you going to raise a child on drug money?"

"My kids are ok."

"But this one won't be."

"This one what?" Oh, wait... Are you pregnant Adara?"

I nodded my head up and down.

"For real bae?" He put his hand on my stomach.

"Yes, for real." I said.

"Oh shit! That's what's up bae come here!" He helped me stand up so he could hug me tight.

"When did you find out?"

"I've known for about a week."

"And you are just now telling me?"

"Yes."

"I told you I was going to get you pregnant, didn't I? That's why you were going off on me like that."

"I was going off because I was mad."

"I know but you have never snapped like you did last night. I see you put my stuff away." he said as he looked towards our bedroom.

"I did." I looked back at the bedroom with him.

"Bae I am going to do what I have to do to make things right for our baby." He had tears in his eyes.

"No more drinking."

"You're right. I need to stop."

"And you need to get a job."

"I know. It's been hard for me because of my background, but I will do what I got to do. Anything for my wife and my baby. I got you. I got us."

Chapter 15

Wes did get a job. I got a new Porsche Cayenne truck. Luckily, I had insurance and good credit. It was time for an upgrade anyways. I helped Wes get a new car. Most women would not do that, but I loved Wes, and I wanted him to have his own. I felt like I was being a good woman by helping him. Plus, I did not want him to be driving my car anymore. He put some money into buying his own car, but the bulk of it came from me. I also helped him get his driver's license, so he would be legit, and I added his car to my insurance. The stuff I did for the love of that man made me shake my head at times. I was doing everything in my power to make that relationship work, and get ready for the new edition to our lives.

Since Wes was working, he wasn't at Quinten's house as much. I thought that he was slowing down on the drinking, but Wes was just finding better and more improved ways to conceal it. I noticed that he started chewing gum, and popping mints more. He started drinking before coming home, and Wes had become a great actor. He would walk in the house putting on a show like he hadn't touched a drop of alcohol. I guess he thought that I wouldn't notice, but I did. My pregnancy had me so sick that I didn't felt like arguing, so I turned a blind eye to it.

I was almost through the first trimester. The doctor told me that things would get better in the second. I prayed for the day that the sickness and nausea would be over. I hadn't been at the shop much because I was too sick. I wasn't sure if I was going to be feeling up to going to Bianca's birthday celebration that was coming up.

I was lying on the couch half asleep when I heard Wes coming in from work.

"Hey bae." he said when he walked in.

"Hey." I groaned.

"Aww look at my baby." He put a bouquet of flowers in front of me. The smell made me feel sick. I slowly sat up. I noticed that he was chewing gum, but I ignored it.

"Thank you." I gave a weak smile. The bouquet was beautiful. It had roses, lilies and orchids. I knew that he spent a lot of money on it, but I was unable enjoy it like I wanted to because was sick.

"Not feeling good?"

"No."

"Aight chill. I am going to take a shower and then I will be back to take care of my baby."

He put the bouquet of flowers on the table and disappeared to the back of our house. Wes came back twenty minutes later. He'd brushed his teeth. I knew that meant that he didn't want me to smell liquor on his breath. He was getting craftier by the day. He smelled good like the Axe soap that he liked to use. My pregnancy wouldn't allow me to enjoy the smell.

"Did you have to swim in the body soap?" I asked.

He laughed at me and sat down.

"Hush beautiful woman."

"I'm just saying."

"You're just pregnant."

I sat back up, so he could sit down.

"Come here." he said and patted his thighs. I laid my head on his lap and faced my head towards the television. I started watching an episode of Black Ink Crew Chicago. He ran his fingers through my hair a few times, then, he massaged my back until I feel asleep.

When I woke up, he'd cooked and cleaned the house. I love a man that can cook. Wes was stepping up again and I was enjoying it.

"Did you sleep ok?" Wes asked.

"Yes."

"Are you feeling better?"

"Yes, I do."

"Good. I hope that you can hold this down. I made you a small plate."

I stood up to go and take a shower and brush my teeth. I returned to the living room in my satin robe, fluffy slippers, and my hair pulled up into a ponytail. He put a plate of warm mashed potatoes and gravy, baked chicken, and cornbread in front of me. His cooking is always delicious, even when it is simple. I ate most of it. Then, I sat back while he cleaned the kitchen, He came back to the couch and sat next to me. I put my feet up on his legs, and told him that I was feeling nauseas again.

He said, "Maybe you should hit this joint. It will knock off some of that nausea."

"I can't do that. I 'm pregnant."

"It will not hurt the baby."

"You don't know that."

"My ex-wife told me that it worked for her." I took the joint from his hand and took a couple of pulls. I blew the smoke out and took a couple more pulls. I passed it back to him, then, leaned my head back on the couch and closed my eyes. After a few minutes, I started to feel better. I heard him put the joint out in the ashtray and then I felt his hands massaging my feet. The feeling made me relax even more, but it also made me feel hot. It had been a while since we'd had sex, and I wanted him to make love to me. I sat up and looked at him.

"What's wrong bae? That doesn't feel good?" he asked.

"No, it feels great, but I want something."

"What? I'll go and get it." he said. I opened my robe to show him my nude body. He looked over at me with devilish grin.

"Oh, you want that?" he asked.

"Um hum."

"Can you handle it?"

"Um hum." I smiled.

"I'll meet you in the bedroom." I stood up and let my robe drop to the floor and walked into the bedroom naked. He turned off the television and followed me.

Wes was so gentle and attentive while making love to me. He was rubbing my hair, and kissing me. I felt his love as he rocked in and out of me at a slow rhythm. It was much different than his usual thug loving style of having sex. I fell in love with him all over again.

Chapter 16

A month later, Wesley lost his job again. We are back to the same old things. I was paying for everything. Wes was sitting at home all day, or at Quinten's house. I had dipped far into my savings account. That was supposed to be my no touch money, and I had been pulling from it a lot. I was running through cash faster than I could make it. Slowly things were starting to go downhill again. I was pregnant and stressing. Wes's bullshit was not making it any better. He wasn't helping me at all, and I started to question why I decided to keep the baby.

Wesley told me that Quinten was trying to get him to hustle again. I didn't want him to hustle. I didn't want to be worried about him getting shot, or going to jail, or the police kicking in my door looking for him. In my opinion, all Wes needed was to get a good job and hold on to it. I started thinking about getting a side hustle going on. I was already selling products in the salon, which was one of my hustles. I had also started my own hair weave line that I was still working on. I had invested a lot of money in my hair extension line and I wasn't sure how it was going to do. My biggest fear was that it was going to be a waste of money, so I started thinking up other side hustles; like also selling Avon or Pleasure Products to make some more money. I heard Bedroom Kandi by Kandi Burruss was a good money maker. I was thinking about getting involved in that movement.

"Yea, but you shouldn't have to do that if you got a grown ass, able body man living up in your house for real cousin." Nikita said. I was doing her hair at the shop. I had just told her about my ideas to get some more cash flow going.

"Girl I know, but he has such a hard time finding a job. I can't depend on him. I have a baby coming." I said. I picked up a section of her hair and used the small curling iron I had in my hand to put a tiny curl in it. I was almost finished curling the back of her head. I was glad because I was ready to sit down before my next client came in.

"All the reason he should be stepping up with his raggedy ass." Nikita said. She was starting to dislike Wes as much as I hated her baby daddy Jakari.

"I know cousin." I said as I turned the swivel chair to the side. She had a bunch of tight curls going across the back of her short haircut. I had put a couple of weave tracks from my new hairline in the top so she could try them out for me.

"I know my baby daddy ain't shit, but at least he works. I hate to see you going through this."

She was right. I couldn't believe that I was going through some of the same stuff that I used to be pissed at her about. She had gone through something similar with Jakari's stupid ass. Before he went to barber school, he was living off Nikita. She was working every day while he stayed home and played video games. It wasn't like he was watching their son because her mom baby sat him during the day. He was just being lazy. Part of me was in denial that Wes was doing the same thing to me. I kept making up excuses for him in my mind, and justifying his reasons for not working. Doing that made me feel better about the situation. I refused to believe that Wes was a fuck boy, although he was showing me fuck boy behavior.

"To top it all off, I feel like Wes may be cheating on me, but I have no proof. He's been coming home late, not answering my calls, keeping his phone on him. Every time I go through his phone, everything is erased."

"He's hiding something. Jakari used to do that same stuff until he got lazy and started forgetting to erase texts. That's how I found out about one of the bitches at the shop."

"Girl don't trip. That man loves you and only you. I doubt that he is doing anything." Bianca said. She was sitting at her station listening to our conversation. She was looking at her phone scrolling through her social media pages. Her next client was scheduled to walk through the door at any minute.

I thought about it for a second. She could be right, but my intuition was telling me something different. My mom always taught me to listen to my intuition. She always said that it is a special gift that God gave women to sense when something was wrong.

"You could be right B." I said to Bianca.

I finished up Nikita's hair and walked her out. I had a few minutes before my next client to sit down and rest my feet. I sat in my swivel chair and rubbed my belly. I was starting to show a little bit.

I had announced my pregnancy to my staff when I returned to the shop after taking a week off during my first trimester. Everyone was beyond excited about my new addition. All my stylists claimed to be my baby's new auntie. Bianca said she couldn't wait. She had plans to spoil my baby. Once all my stylists knew about my pregnancy, they all went out of their way to do things for me, and make sure that I was comfortable. I loved the attention.

Bianca walked over to my station after coming from the break room. She handed me a bowl of fruit and told me that it was for the baby.

"Well what about me?" I asked.

"It's for you too, but my cute little niece or nephew needs it more." I laughed, so she laughed. "You know I am just kidding sis. I will be right back."

Bianca stepped outside to smoke a cigarette. I wished that I could have a cigarette. I had finally kicked my habit for my baby. I refused to be one of those mothers who smoked their whole pregnancy. I was too worried about my baby's health. Bianca came back in a few minutes later and sat down in the chair next to mine.

"So now that the baby is coming, when is the wedding?"

"I don't know yet. I haven't really had the chance to plan."

"Let me know when you start the planning process, I am a great wedding planner and I can help bring your vision to life, and I can throw you an amazing bridal shower and bachelorette party."

"Aight sis." I smiled.

"You and Wes are still coming to my birthday party, right?"

"Yes, we will be there."

"Good. You guys are such a cute couple sis. I am praying that things work out for you two. You don't see too many successful black relationships or marriages these days so I am cheering for y'all."

"Thank you. What's up with your boo?"

"I don't know. I think I am going to end it with him after my birthday."

"Why?"

"Well, you know that we are not official yet. We are still just dating. I feel like it has been a year now, so he should know by now if I am the one that he wants to be with. I don't know if he is dealing with other women, but I can only guess that he is. I am just tired of waiting around for him."

"I feel you sis. At the end of the day, you have to do what makes you happy."

"Exactly."

"On another note. Is Deon coming to your party?"

"I don't know. Why?"

"I was asking for a friend."

"Oh, you know somebody who wants to get with him?"

"Maybe."

"Who?"

None of your business." I laughed. I was lying. I was checking to see if Deon was going to her party for my sake. I know how Wes gets about Deon. If I had to, I would orchestrate a way to get there and leave before Deon showed up.

"Here comes your client." Bianca said and stood up.

"I swear this chick better not get on my nerves today." I said.

Bianca laughed and took my bowl of fruit. She walked to the back to put it on my desk in my office. I stood up to walk over and greet my client at the door.

***

When I walked into the house from the shop, Wes was sitting on the couch in his pajama pants and no shirt. Wes was sexy to me, even when he was not trying. He was chewing on a piece of gum and watching a Chris Tucker movie.

"We need to talk Wes."

"Ok. Hi. How are you doing?" he said sarcastically.

"Hi Wes."

"Hi Adara. Sup?"

I sat down next to him and looked him in his eyes.

"Why am I wearing this ring if we are never going to get married?"

"What are you talking about? We are going to get married. Why are you looking so stressed? You are too beautiful to be looking like that."

"I am stressed Wes."

"Why?" Because of my job situation, right?"

"Yes Wes. I feel like you're very lax when it comes to employment. I have been taking care of both of us, and we need to be getting ready for this baby. I am running through my money, and I have started tapping into funds that I wasn't supposed to be touching to hold you down."

"You know that it is hard for me to get a job, but when I have one I got you."

"I know, but the reality is, you have two children Wes and one on the way, and I am not seeing your motivation to really get up, get out, and get something."

"Ok, I hear you Adara. I got this." Wes responded.

It irritated me that Wes gave me the response I expected. I was trying to have a sincere conversation with him about our situation, and he wasn't giving me anything, but the same old lines. I took a breath and changed the subject.

"Bianca's party is this weekend."

"Aight." His eyes were back on the television.

"No more drinking."

Aight." He said without breaking his focus on the television. I took the remote for him and turned the television off.

"Adara." he said.

"Look at me Wes." He looked at me.

"I hear you."

"I'm serious Wes."

Aight."

"Please be on your best behavior."

"I will."

I knew that was a lie as soon as it came out of his mouth. I knew that I was going to be babysitting him. Which meant that I was going to be driving, and I was not going to have a good time. I missed the days when I wasn't responsible for a grown ass adult. I hated that I had to be the responsible person all the time because Wes didn't know his limits. I ended the conversation, and I stood up to walk to the kitchen. I made dinner, ate, and went to bed. Wesley came to bed later and curled up next to me.

"I love you. I don't know what I would do without you." he whispered.

Chapter 17

Wes surprisingly held himself together at Bianca's party, but, with my supervision. I was on top of everything that he had in his cup most of the night accept the few times that I went to the bathroom. I wished that I could have made him come to the bathroom with me every time. If I could have picked him up and put him into my pocket, it would have been even better. It was ridiculous that I felt that way, but I did.

Nothing changed with Wesley. He held it together for Bianca's party. I was thanking God that he did not embarrass me. After Bianca's party, it was back to the same old things. I was very clear when I told Wes that there was to be no more drinking, and he just kept taking my kindness for weakness. He kept drinking and hanging out with Quinten. He continued to try to hide it from me by chewing gum, popping mints, and brushing his teeth. Drinking orange soda to kill the smell seemed to be his new thing to do right before walking in the door.

It was close to midnight and I had called Wes at least ten times with no response. I was boiling hot. I swear I could feel my blood bubbling in my veins. I called him one last time. I was in the middle of my second trimester, and I wasn't in the mood for his bullshit. I snatched my keys and purse off the table, slipped on my sneakers, and headed to Quinten's house.

I pulled up to his cousins house a short time later. I jumped out of my truck and walked up wearing a grey jogging suit with the hooded sweatshirt unzipped, and a fitted whited t-shirt. My baby bump was protruding, my hair was in a ponytail, and I had no make-up on my face. Wes, Quinten, another guy, and a couple of girls were all sitting on the porch smoking and drinking. A look of shock covered Wes's face when he saw me.

He shook his head and said, "Don't come over here on that bullshit Adara."

I stepped to him and said, "You can't answer your phone?"

"I didn't know that you were calling."

"Maybe you didn't know that I was calling because you got this shit in your hand!" I snatched the bottle out of his hand threw it off the porch. It shattered on the ground.

Wes jumped up and yelled, "Yo! What the fuck is your problem!"

Quinten grabbed him and said, "Chill out."

"My problem is you! I asked you to not be drinking!" I yelled. I was probably making myself look crazy in front everyone else on the porch. I didn't care. I was pissed.

"I'm a grown ass man! I can do what I want to do!"

"Not at my house you won't! If you want to drink, do that shit right here where you are!"

I bruised his ego and his pride when I said that in front of everybody. I knew I was being disrespectful, but at that point, I was too far gone to catch myself. I was just saying what was on my mind with no filter. He instantly blew up.

"Yo! Who are you talking to like that!" he yelled and stormed towards me with his fists balled up. His eyes were bloodshot red. I stepped back, and his cousin intervened.

"Yo cuz. Chill out." Quinten put his hand on Wes's chest.

"I'm telling you now Adara, get the fuck out of here!" he jumped towards me.

"What? You tryna put your hands on me Wesley!?"

"Adara go home. I got him." Quinten said calmly and took a sip of beer.

"Quinten, you are foul as hell because you know that I'm pregnant, and you over here drinking with him. You know how he gets!"

"Yo cuz go in the house so I can talk to her."

Wes walked into the house and slammed the door.

Quinten walked with me to my truck. I apologized to him for causing a ruckus at his house. I explained what I had been going through with Wes and he understood.

"Look go home. I'll keep him here. Aye and you can't be coming over here turning up and shit. My house is hot, I got drugs here. You feel me?"

I nodded my head. He smiled and hugged me. "Your ass is crazy. Out here pregnant and turning up. Go home."

I got into my car and went home.

***

The next morning, I heard keys in the door as I was getting back into my bed. I had just finished brushing my teeth. I pulled my blanket over my lap, and picked up a book from my nightstand. I had been reading the book for a few days and was trying to finish it. I rolled my eyes when Wes came into the room. He walked back out of the room and walked into the bathroom. I listened to him emptying his bladder. I'm sure that it was all the liquor from the night before. I heard him wash his hands, brush his teeth, and wash his face. Then, he came back into the bedroom. He stood at the foot of the bed and asked, "Why did you do that last night?"

"I have nothing to say to you." I kept my eyes on my book.

"You were out of control and disrespectful." he said.

"I was out of control?" I asked. I had a screwed face when I looked up from my book I rolled my eyes and looked back down at my book. *He has got to be crazy to think I am going to feel bad about going off on him last night.* I thought.

I refused to back down. In my mind, he had me hell of fucked up. He walked over to me and snatched the book out of my hand and slammed it on the nightstand. I frowned and looked up at him. He still reeked of alcohol and I was sure that he was still drunk.

"You were Adara!" He hit a nerve when he snatched my book and slammed it. I had to stop myself from snapping on him. I spoke calmly and with a low tone of voice.

"How many times have I asked you not to drink? How many times have we talked about you coming home late? How many times have we argued about you not answering the phone? You continue to do the same things and I am sick of it. What if I did that stuff to you Wes?"

"It doesn't matter how many times we have talked about it. It doesn't give you the right to come over someone else's house tripping!" he said angrily. His voice was escalated, and that was it for me. I couldn't stay calm. I fell right into the argument that Wes was looking for. I gave him what he wanted.

"Q is family!" I yelled.

"So!" Wes yelled back.

"I am pregnant! I shouldn't have to come over there looking for you Wesley! I called you ten times! What if something was wrong!? You wouldn't have known because you were too busy drinking!"

"I don't give a fuck! I can drink what I want! When I want! You can't do shit about it! You ain't my mom Adara! You can't control what the fuck I do!"

"You're a grown ass boy!" I yelled at him. I was firing verbal shots. He wanted to take me there, so he got me there. I was popping off left and right again with no filter.

"Fuck you Adara!"

"Fuck me Wes!? Fuck you! I'm about to be raising a child! I shouldn't have to be running around here chasing you while you are trying to find yourself at the bottom of a bottle! If you want to act like a child, then maybe you need to go back to your mama so she can finish raising you cause I ain't going to do it!"

"You a Bitch!" he yelled and walked out of the room.

"Bitch!?" I yelled. I jumped out of bed and followed him into the living room. "Did you just disrespect me in my own house!?"

"I call it how I see it!"

"Get the fuck out of my house right now!" I stood in front of him and pointed my finger towards the door.

"I ain't going nowhere!"

"Get out Wesley! Now!"

He stood with his arms crossed while glaring at me. "You better back the fuck up off me Adara! I telling you."

"Or what? Your gonna hit me? Like you threatened me last night?! I'm calling your cousin!"

"Don't call my people!"

I walked away from him with my phone to my ear. I walked downstairs to the laundry room.

"Hello Quinten. Can you come and get your cousin! He is tripping and I want him out of my house now before I call the police on him!" He stormed down the stairs and into the laundry room where I was standing.

"You think this is a fucking game Adara! I told you not to call him!

"See Quinten come now!" I said into the phone. Wes grabbed my arm with all his strength and yanked the phone from my hands.

"Don't grab me like that! I'm pregnant Wes!" I yelled and snatched my arm out of his grip.

"Don't come over here cuz!" he yelled into the phone. He hung up and threw my phone at the wall. It shattered and fell to the ground. I took off running back up the stairs and into my room. I locked myself in my bedroom.

I heard him answer his phone and then he began pounding on the door. "Adara! Open this door!"

Suddenly, he stopped pounding. I heard him go outside. A few minutes later I heard the front door open again. "Adara, it's me Quinten." I opened the door.

"I got him. You alright?"

"Yes. I don't want him back over here." I said.

"Did he put his hands on you?"

"No, he just grabbed my arm, but it scared me."

Quinten shook his head and said, "He is probably still gone off that Hennessy from last night. I'm sorry fam I didn't know that he was this bad. I'mma talk to him because he is gonna have to slow down if he is doing all this. You got his stuff?"

I quickly packed a duffle bag full of Wes's things and gave it to Quinten.

"Aight I got him, he can stay at my house for a while. I'll check on you later."

"Ok." I followed Quinten to the door and locked it after he walked out. I watched him argue with Wes before they pulled off.

"Cuz get into my car. You can come back and get your car when you sober up." Quinten said. Wes gave

Quinten a few reasons why he should drive and then he got into Quinten's car. I watched them pull off and I went to go find my phone. Thank God that it hadn't broke, the back and the battery had been separated from the phone. I picked up the pieces and put it back together. The first call I made was to Nikita.

***

I had a lock smith come and change the locks again. Nikita came over to chill with me for a few hours because I was scared. I didn't know what Wes was going to do when he came back. Knowing him he wouldn't be sober when he did show back up. I also called Chanel to tell her what happened. She was angry and told me that she would be in town the following weekend to visit.

Wes showed up later that night. When he realized that his key wouldn't work, he began knocking and pounding on the door.

"Go away Wes!" I yelled through the door. Nikita watched him through my window blinds.

"You changed the locks!?" he yelled. The slur of his words told me that he was drunk. I knew he wouldn't return without alcohol in his system.

"Leave!" I yelled.

"No! I want my shit!"

I looked at Nikita. "Should I open it?" I whispered.

"Hell no." she whispered back to me.

"I already gave you your shit Wes!"

"I want the rest of my shit! Open this fucking door Adara and quit playing with me!"

"I'm going to call the police!" I yelled through the door.

I don't give a fuck! Call 'em!" he started trying to kick the door in.

"Wes Stop!"

"Open this fucking door!"

"No!"

Nikita walked away from the blinds and over to the table to pick up her purse. She had her gun in it. If Wes came through the door, she was going to light him up. She walked back over to the blinds with her purse in hand.

BOOM! BOOM! The door shook. I thought that it was going to burst open, so I stepped back a little. I was sure that the neighbors could hear what was going on. I was embarrassed.

"Wes Stop!"

"Girl he is tripping. Call the police." Nikita said.

I called and said, "My boyfriend is trying to break into my house." I gave them the address and disconnected the call.

"The police are on the way!" I yelled through the door.

"Aye yo! Fuck you aight!" he yelled, then, he turned and walked away. He got into his car and pulled off. Nikita's eyebrows were raised. She had never seen Wes drunk and belligerent.

"Girl he is crazy." she said.

I shook my head. I didn't know what to say. The police arrived minutes later and took my report while a few neighbors watched from their porches. They encouraged me to file a restraining order. I heard them, but I didn't do it. I loved Wes. I just wished that he would stop drinking, and get it together. When he wasn't drinking, he was a great guy, but the drinking enhanced his temper and brought out the worst in him. Nikita helped me pack an overnight bag. She offered her house for me to stay for a little while until things cooled down. I appreciated her, but there was no way that I was going to stay anywhere near her fuck boy, when I was trying to get away from my own. I declined and rented a room at the Marriot.

Part of me believed that Wes would change. I felt that if he had a steady job, he wouldn't be hanging out and drinking as much. He always seemed to be more focused when he was working. That was what I kept telling myself.

I was too in love with Wes to deal with the reality of everything. The reality was he was still drinking even when he was working. Wes's drinking was a problem, and his temper was a problem. Both problems that would probably take more than me wishing, praying, and complaining to fix. I was way beyond reality. I had created my own excuses for him to deal with his madness. Little did I know, there was more to come.

Chapter 18

I wasn't ready for the next day at the salon. I don't think anyone was ready for the next day at the salon. It was crazy busy. We were booked up all day. Every stylist's chair was filled, and we kept getting walk-in's. It was good for business, but I was mentally and emotionally drained because of Wes. I was tired and I didn't feel like being there. It didn't help that the baby growing inside of me was draining every, last, ounce of energy out of me. I wasn't in the mood for anymore drama, but more drama was on the way.

I was finishing up with my last client when she walked in. She was short, skinny, and light skinned. She had long, sandy brown hair, and big eyes. I saw her ask my receptionist a question. My receptionist nodded her head and walked over to get me. I told my client that I would be right back.

"Hi!" I said when I approached her.

She responded, but not with a smile. She was holding a baby in her arms.

"Cute baby. How may I help you?"

"My name is Raven. This is Wesley's daughter Sierra." She said. I looked at the baby again. She had to be a year old. I was stunned and speechless. The look on my face must have told her that I knew nothing about the information she had just given me.

"He didn't tell you, right?" she asked.

"Um, can we step outside and talk?" I said. I wasn't sure if any of my staff heard what she said, but I didn't want them to hear anything else.

"Sure." She followed me outside. She looked to be a couple of years younger than Wesley and me.

Once we were outside, I said, "It is nice to meet you Raven. Wes has never mentioned you, or a baby to me."

"I heard that he was messing with you through a friend. She comes here to get her hair done. He never told me about you. He disappeared right after I told him that I was pregnant. He blocked me from his phone and social media. Then, my friend told me that he was not claiming our baby and that he had gotten engaged to you."

That wasn't the type of news that I wanted to hear. Especially after the kind of night that I had with Wes. I could feel a headache forming. I kept my cool. She wasn't being disrespectful, so there was no reason for me to turn up. *Here we go again. Another female and another baby that Wes never told me about.* I thought. His nerve to be disclaiming the beautiful little girl was just baffling to me. I was standing there tongue-tied. I couldn't figure out how to respond.

"I apologize for coming up to your place of business with this drama. I just didn't know any other way to get in touch with him. All I want him to do is get a paternity test to prove that she is his, and if he chooses to have nothing to do with her after that, I am fine with it." Raven said.

I said, "I apologize for what he has put you through. I honestly didn't know anything and if I did, I surely would have encouraged him to be a part of his daughter's life."

"It's ok. You were the only way that I knew that I could get a hold of him. I don't know any of his family."

"Can I hold her?" I asked.

"Sure." She handed the little girl to me. She was a very pretty baby. A lighter version of Wesley.

"She is beautiful." I said.

"Thank you." She smiled. She looked down at my belly and asked, "Are you pregnant?"

"Yes I am." I said and looked down at my belly. After holding her for a few minutes, I handed the little girl back to her.

"Can I give you my number to give to him?" she asked.

"Yes, and I will make sure that he calls you."

"Thank you." she said. I saved her phone number in my cell phone.

"How far along are you?" she asked.

"Five months."

"I wish you all the best with your baby. Wesley is a trip girl."

"Don't I know it."

"Thank you. It was nice meeting you." she said.

Raven left and I went back into the shop. I felt sick to my stomach Every time I looked up, it was something else with Wes. Baby's mom number two, child number three, and I was having a child with him. Which made me baby's mom number three; having child number four for Wesley. A strong feeling of regret consumed me. "Why?" I asked myself as I finished up my client. I walked my client out and headed to my office in the back of the salon.

Why had I made the decision to keep my baby instead of getting an abortion as Nikita suggested. It was too late for me to turn back. My baby was growing inside of me, and I was stuck with my decision. I had to deal with the circumstances the best way that I could. "Ugh I am done with Wesley." I said to myself as I paced back and forth in my office. Bianca came back to my office to check on me.

"Are you ok girl?" she asked.

"Yes I am."

"Who was that?" she asked.

"She was an old friend of mine." I said. I lied. I had to. I couldn't tell her that Wes had another baby. I was embarrassed about it.

"Oh ok. Her baby was cute."

"I know. She really was."

"Do you need anything sis?" Bianca asked me. Something told me that she didn't believe a word that was coming out of my mouth. I wondered if she had overheard the conversation and was just playing along with my lie.

"No, I am ok."

"Alright. Well just let me know." she said.

"Ok." She walked out and left me in my office. I sat back there for a little longer to get myself mentally prepared for my next client.

***

I made it back to the hotel later that evening. I called Chanel and she said that she would stop by to spend some time with me.

"Look at you belly." she said when I let her in my hotel suite.

"I know."

"How's pregnancy?"

"Well, now that the first trimester is over I can live a little, but I am still very tired."

She sat down on the couch and asked, "Where's Nikita's ghetto ass tonight?"

"I didn't invite her."

"Why?"

"Because I am not in the mood to hear you two bickering."

"That is usually her."

"No, that is you too and most of the time you start it. Do you always have to throw shade? So, what that she doesn't wear designer stuff. She is family."

"She is ratchet."

"She is your family too so stop sis."

"Technically she is not."

"Ok, but you have been knowing her the same amount of time that you've been knowing me. That is a lifetime." Chanel rolled her eyes and put her Gucci clutch purse on the coffee table. I looked at her perfectly manicured nails and toes and remembered that I needed to get mine done.

"I'm dating someone." she said.

"Really? Who is he?"

"I don't want to jinx it so I am not going to tell you."

"That's not right sis. I guess I will just have to get my detective work on." Chanel laughed.

"I will tell you when the time is right. I will say this; he is a really nice guy and I really like him."

"Um hum. That smile on your face must mean that he is good in bed."

"Amazing." she giggled. "That is all you get."

"Tell me more" I begged.

"Nope. Anyways. How are you doing sis?" she asked. I guess she figured she would just change the subject before I forced her to tell me everything that I wanted to know about the mystery man in her life.

"I am alright considering the reason why I am here in this suite."

"Has he called since last night?"

"A million times."

"Why don't you just block him?"

"I don't know. Because part of me just wishes that he would do right." My voice started cracking and my eyes began to water as I continued to speak, "I love him, but I am tired of the bullshit. I see good in him, even though he does some fucked up shit sometimes sis." I used my finger to catch my tears before they fell.

"Yea but what are you going to do? Wait for him to change?" she asked.

"I don't know, and a girl came up to the shop today with a child that is supposed to be his."

"Please tell me that you are lying."

"I'm not sis. It happened before we got together, but I feel like why do I have to get information from everyone else, but not from the person I'm sleeping with?"

"I told you he wasn't going to be worth your time." She said and flipped her long, jet-black, tresses off her shoulder.

"Sis don't start with the I told you so's right now."

She scratched her scalp and said, "Alright. Well, is there anything that I can do to help?"

My pride wouldn't let me tell her that I had fell behind on a few bills. I had already decided that I would have to figure it out. I did want to burden her and I was too embarrassed about where I was at financially because of Wes. Plus, I was staying in an expensive hotel, instead of my home because of the same person. I knew that I could have chosen a cheaper place to lay my head, but my fear of bed bugs, and soiled bedding wouldn't allow me to.

"No sis I am ok." I said.

"Well you know what they say. You can't raise a man." Chanel said.

"Right."

Chapter 19

"I want to come home. I miss you."

"You called me out of my name Wesley and disrespect is something that I cannot and will not tolerate."

"I know bae and I apologize."

"I don't want to hear it."

"I was tripping bae. I was still mad about you showing up to Quinten's house acting crazy. That doesn't make what I did right, and I know that. I was out of pocket for disrespecting you."

"I just can't deal with you."

"Come on Adara. It's me Wesley. You know me. You know that I love you to death. I can't live without you.

"At this point, Wes, I am not so sure I want to do this anymore."

"So, you're going to leave me? Right now, Adara? What about our baby? I can't lose you and our baby. Adara I need you. I ain't going to do right without you.

"You haven't been doing right with me Wes."

"Baby please."

"No. Why didn't you tell me about your daughter?"

"My what?"

"Your daughter. Your ex Raven came to my shop with the little girl looking for you. How tacky to have a chick coming to me about you. At my place of business of all places Wes."

"Hol'up, that chick told me that she didn't know if she was pregnant or not. I wasn't the only dude she was fucking with either."

"So, deny the baby?"

"I didn't deny shit! I didn't even know about any baby Adara!"

"Why wouldn't you check into it?"

"I swear Adara, I was just fucking that girl when I first came home from prison. She was just a jump off. When I got with you I lost contact with that chick."

"She said you blocked her from everything."

"For real Adara? You gonna believe that chick over me? Like I said she was a hoe and she was messing with other dudes at the time. She probably doesn't know whose baby that is for real!"

"Well she wants a paternity test."

"Fine. Whatever man. Now can I come home? I've been gone for two months. I am tired of being away of my fiancé and my baby."

"No Wes. You are not working and I am not dealing with your drinking problem."

"I have a job now. I am focused baby. I promise."

***

"Girl Jakari didn't come home last night." Nikita said.

I was sitting with Nikita in the waiting area of the nail salon. We were waiting for a nail tech to call us over for pedicures. My stomach was so big that I could no longer do my own. I couldn't even see my feet. It is going to feel so good to put my feet into some warm water and get a foot massage.

"Shut up." I said and looked at her.

"Girl yes. His ass walked in the house at five am talking about he went out and was too drunk to drive, so he spent the night at his best friend's house."

"Girl stop. I can't."

"I liked to have slapped him silly. Now, I see some pictures on Instagram of him and that girl at the shop. You know I am about ready to go up there and whoop her ass. I haven't been feeling right either and I am praying that this boy hasn't given me something."

I shook my head. Jakari dirty dick ass needs to be slapped silly. He been running around on my cousin for the longest. He has no respect for Nikita at all, but how could I say anything when I let Wes move back home with me.

Wes asked me to come back home several times, and I told him that he couldn't repeatedly. After a while, I stopped believing that I really wanted him to stay away. I told myself that I didn't want to do the rest of my pregnancy alone. I told myself that I hated sleeping alone. I told myself that I missed his kiss, his touch, and his voice. I told myself that I missed him holding me at night. I told myself that I missed making love to him, and that I didn't want to start over with someone else. I made myself believe that I needed him just as much as he needed me, so I told Wes that he could move back home.

Wes wasted no time moving back home. He came home on his best behavior, but I questioned how long his good behavior was going to last. It felt good to have him home again. I missed being wrapped up in his muscular arms at night as we slept. His lips felt softer than before when he kissed me. It was great to hear him compliment me and tell me that he loved me repeatedly throughout the day. When Wes kissed my stomach, and talked to the baby, I fell back in love with him. I prayed that it would last forever this time, but my prayers went unanswered. His promises were not kept. Some time went by and he was back to the same old bullshit again. This time, his alcohol problem, his temper, and his insecurities reached a whole new level. He did have a job, and that was about the only good he had going on.

I found myself calling him repeatedly at night because he would leave work, and then go straight to hang out with Quinten until late hours. He would answer the phone, but he would always give me an excuse. Sometimes he would keep telling me that he would be home in an hour, until one hour turned into three hours. Then, the arguing started back up. There were nights when I felt like he would start an argument with me just so he could have a reason to snap and hang up on me.

Wes also didn't tell me that his job was only temporary until the assignment ended. I knew that I should have done a bit more probing on the job situation. I made Wes contact Raven, and the paternity test proved that he was the father of her daughter Simone. Which meant Wes had three mouths to feed plus the one coming. I was very frustrated about it, but there was nothing that I could do. It happened before me, and my baby was coming.

Once that job assignment was over, the drinking flared back up, and he started questioning me more about my whereabouts. He'd snatched my phone out of my hand several times to see who I was text messaging. He started accusing me of being sneaky and talking to other men. I had to explain to him several times that he had nothing to worry about. I was a walking balloon. No one was thinking about trying to be with me, and I wasn't trying to deal with anybody. Especially since I had a whole human being growing inside of me. Wes knew that I had been loyal to him since day one, so I wasn't sure where the new suspicions were coming from. Wes was the one with the suspicious actions.

"What have I gotten myself back into?" I asked myself many times. It was the same cycle over, and over again. He would do something, I would fuss, we would argue, we would make up, and then it would start over. I was tired of it.

In retrospect, I guess I wasn't tired enough because I was steadily holding on to Wes and dealing with it. No matter how crazy it got between us, I kept making excuses up in my head for the reason why I would stay with him. I kept giving him more chances in anticipation that a change would come. As things got worse, I started to realize that the change may not ever come. Just like Chanel said.

I thought about the last argument that I had with Wes as I sat next to my cousin in the lobby of the nail salon. I looked at Nikita with my eye brows up. "Cousin, why do you put up with Jakari?" I asked.

"Because I love him. I've been with Jakari for seven years. I can't see myself being with anyone else."

"But why deal with all the disrespect? Jakari is a fuck-boy. Don't you think that you can do better?"

"And what? Start over with someone else who will probably do the same thing? I already know Jakari and what he is going to do."

"All men are not fuck-boy's Nikita. There is a good man out there. So, you are willing to let a man cheat on you, disrespect you, and verbally abuse you because you don't want to start over? You're telling me that you are ok with Jakari possibly giving you AIDS too if it came down to it because you love him? Have you ever thought that being alone may be better than dealing with some raggedy ass man?"

"Look who's talking." Nikita said.

"I know but Wes isn't cheating on me."

"Not that you know of. Wes is a Fuck Boy too, so why are you still dealing with him?"

"Because I need to be telling myself the same thing that I am telling you."

***

I enjoyed spending time with my cousin Nikita at the nail shop. I was feeling good until I walked in the house. Wes got to tripping over nothing. I was never in the mood for whatever new person he was going to be from day to day. All I had been thinking about was having my baby so I could have my body back, and see my little girl.

"Where the fuck you been all day Adara?" Wes asked me when I walked into the door. He was sitting on the couch with the remote in his hand as usual.

"With Nikita." I said as I walked towards the kitchen.

"All day?"

"Yes, and I stopped by the store to grab some milk." I held the gallon of milk I had in my hand up in the air so he could see it.

"Don't be lying to me yo!" he said as he stood up. and started walking towards me.

I paused and looked at him. "Have you been drinking?" I asked.

"What does that matter?"

"Cause you're acting crazy Wes." I said. I guessed that he was the paranoid drunk this night. I wasn't in the mood to deal for his suspicions and all the colorful cheating scenarios that he would come up with to accuse me of.

"So, what that I've had a beer or two. Am I an alcoholic now?"

"You've had more than a beer Wes. I hate when you act like this."

"Let me find out."

"Let you find out what?"

"That you are fucking around on me."

"Are you serious? Do you see my big ass belly? I barely want to mess around with you. Carry your ass on somewhere."

"Let me smell your pussy." Wes said.

"Boy please. If you don't get up out of my face with that."

"Let me smell it. It better not, smell like condoms either." He grabbed my pants.

"Wes get up out of my face with that bullshit!" I pushed his hand off me. His breath smelled like whatever he was drinking, and I didn't feel like dealing with his drunk ass nonsense.

"You ain't gonna let me smell you pussy? You got me fucked up yo."

"You got yourself fucked up Wes."

"You're not going out with Nikita, or Bianca's hoe ass's anymore!"

"What does Bianca have to do with anything? You don't need to be worried about my friends. You need to be worried about finding a job."

"That's what you on! I bring money into this mutha fucka!"

"You think drug money is going to last? Are you trying to go back to prison?"

I don't know why I was letting Wes pull me into an argument. I already knew how Wes could get while under the influence of alcohol. By the way his eyes were glossed over and how slow he was moving, I figured he might have been leaning as well.

"It's gonna last as long as I want it to! You ain't ever satisfied!"

"I'm not about to argue with you Wes."

"Fuck you!" he yelled and walked out; slamming the door behind him. I felt tears began to burn my eyes. I leaned over the kitchen sink and cried. I was about to have a baby soon, and he was arguing with me about stupid shit. I started asking myself why was I trying to make it work with Wes, and if being with him was worth all the stuff he was putting me through. I called Chanel and she consoled me without saying anything negative. I was still upset when I went to bed later that night. I heard Wes come in late that night drunk, leaning, or rolling. He came in the bedroom once and looked at me. I guess to see if I was sleep or not. I heard him walking around the house mumbling stuff and then he passed out on the couch.

***

As time went on, my nervousness grew whenever Wes came home under the influence. I remember times when I couldn't sleep unless he was lying next to me. That turned into feeling like I couldn't sleep when he was in the house drunk. His actions were unpredictable, and I was never sure what person I was going to get when he walked in the door. I didn't know if he was going to be angry, suspicious, or emotional. The last time he came in he was crying and begging me not to leave him. Telling me how much he loved me and needed me. Told me that he knew that he was a fuck up, and that he really wanted to change. He said he didn't know why he did the things he did, and that he'd been praying that God would help him. I couldn't do anything but hold him and promise that I wasn't going to leave. Then, he turned around and cursed me out a few nights later.

Wes had never put his hands on me, but some days I was starting to wonder if he would. I prayed many times that he would not try to attack me with our baby in my stomach. If he did, I didn't want to end up killing his ass trying to protect myself, and end up in prison for the rest of my life. My mom told me that you can't trust someone who is under the influence because they don't know what they are doing. I decided that if he touched me, I was going to fuck him up. I'd picked out my weapons. The lamp that was next to my bed, my stiletto heels that were on my shoe rack, and I had hidden a bat in the closet by the front door.

If I had to go there, I had plenty of knives in the kitchen. The only thing I didn't have was a gun, and I went back and forth in my head a few times about buying one just in case. One would think, that after thinking about all that, I would have left Wes or told him to get out. No, not me. I was willing to risk being on the Snapped television show just to make it work with my fuck boy.

***

The next morning, I felt him crawl into the bed and curl up next to me. I felt my skin crawl.

"Get away from me Wes."

"Why?"

"Because you were disrespectful last night."

"When?"

"You don't remember, right?"

"Bae I don't."

"Move." I pushed him back.

"Stop bae I wanna hold you and my baby."

"Me and the baby don't want to be held."

"Stop being mean. I am sorry for whatever I said or did."

"You are always sorry Wes. I am going to start recording you, so you can see yourself. Maybe that will snap you into reality."

"Don't do that."

"I am, because obviously, you don't realize that you have a drinking and drug problem."

"Don't talk to me like I'm a patient Adara. I'm good. Let me hit it from the side."

"No. You think that I am going to let you get some after you told me fuck me last night? You got, me, you, and the baby messed up. I am telling you Wes if you don't get it together soon, I am about to be done."

"You ain't never going anywhere. I told you before that you are mine and you're stuck with me. You're having my baby. It will be a cold day in hell before you leave me." He looked at his phone and said, "Shit I got to go."

"Where are, you going?"

"I got something to take care of. I'll be back."

He took a shower, got dressed, and kissed me while he was brushing his hair.

"I'll be home later." he said as he was walking out of the door.

"No drinking!" I yelled.

Chapter 20

I was up late again; calling Wes to see where he was at. He was answering the phone when he felt like it. Would tell me that he would be home soon, but never show up. I called him one last time at around two o'clock in the morning. I gave up and went to sleep.

Wes came home around three o'clock in the morning. He got into the bed with me instead of passing out on the couch. He didn't mess with me or try to get any like he usually did. He was still asleep when I left out to go to the shop a few hours later. I had an early client. I was trying to fit all my clients in before I went on maternity leave. I needed the money. Plus, I wanted to make sure my clients were straight before I would be gone for a few months. My stomach was so big that I looked like I was ready to pop. I was about to have my baby girl any day. Lord only knows that I was ready. I didn't feel like being on my feet at the shop that day, but I had to do what I had to do.

As I pulled up I could see that there were a few clients at the shop already. One of them was outside smoking a cigarette. Nikita was inside sitting at my station waiting on me. Bianca and my other stylists had clients in their chairs, and Deon was doing a haircut on one of his clients. I got my big ass out of my truck and walked up.

"Hello." I spoke to the client that was outside smoking the cigarette. I wondered if she was my early client.

"Are you Adara?" she asked.

"Yes I am. Can I help you?"

"Are you still messing with Wesley?" she asked with an attitude. She took another puff of her cigarette and threw it out into the street.

"Excuse me? Who are you?" I asked.

"I am Lesley and I want to know are you still messing with Wesley?"

"Yes, we are in a relationship."

Before I could get another word out of my mouth, she said, "Well he told me that he wasn't fucking with you anymore, and I'm trying to figure out why you are calling my man at all hours of the night?"

"Your man?" I chuckled. *This chick had to be smoking more than cigarettes coming up to my shop telling me that Wesley is her man.* I thought.

"Yes, my man." she said with a roll of her neck. I looked her over. I realized that Wesley had a type of girl that he likes. He had a thing for light skinned girls. The chick was light skin. Just like me, his ex-wife, and his other baby mom. The only difference was that this chick was hood. She had three piercings in her face alone. She had an eye brow piercing, a nose piercing, and a lip piercing. Then she had the nerve to have a piecing in her tongue. I could only imagine all the other piercing that she probably had.

It was nearing the end of winter so it was still chilly outside, so this chick had a hoodie on over a t-shirt. She had the sleeves rolled up. Both of her arms were covered in tattoos. She was rocking a pair of skinny leg jeans and some Jordan's. She had her natural hair pulled up into a ponytail. Her nails were long and busy with multiple colors, and lots of little trinkets on them. I thought I saw Bugs Bunny on one of them. Her eyes were bloodshot red as if she had just smoked a whole blunt to herself, and she had a lot of attitude.

This bitch wants to fight me. I thought. I could tell by her stance that she was ready to swing off at any time, and she could see I was with child. I had on a tight sweater dress with a pair of leggings, so my stomach was visible. She didn't give a fuck if I was pregnant. She was about that street shit. Although I consider myself to be classy, I can throw hands, but not with a baby in my stomach. She had full advantage, and she looked like she was ready to take it. I started mentally preparing myself just in case the chick swung off on me. Because winter was almost over, the snow was melting, but there were still chunks of ice in different places on the sidewalk. I knew that there was a possibility that I could slip and bust my ass trying to fight this chick. I was going to give it all I had.

"Well I don't see how he is yours when you can see that I am very pregnant with his child, wearing his engagement ring, and we live together." I said.

"Bitch, how does he live with you when he has been at my house every day for the past four months? I've been giving him money to give to you to help your broke ass out and shit."

"First, bitch you don't know me. I got money. You've been giving him money to help his broke ass out. Second, he is at my house sleeping right now."

"Whatever. He told me that he was at his cousins, so stay the fuck away from my man!"

Bianca and Nikita overheard the conversation, so they walked outside to see what was going on.

"What's going on cuz?" Nikita asked.

"Yea sis." Bianca said.

"Nothing this bitch was just leaving."

"Like I said, don't call him no more."

"Hol'up I don't know who you are, but I'll beat the breaks off your ass. I ain't pregnant." Nikita said as she stepped in front of me. Nikita is usually a swing first and talk later kind of chick, so I was surprised that she said that much. The chick backed up and started walking away.

"Yea whatever. Wes is my man and if you don't leave him alone, I'll be back." Nikita started going towards her, but I grabbed her shirt and pulled her back.

"Nah don't do that cousin. Not in front of the business. Let her go."

"Yea, but that bitch is disrespectful." Nikita said.

"For real!" Bianca said.

"Wes is fucking around? Oh, hell nah cousin I knew it. I knew it when you told me that he was acting funny with his phone."

"I didn't think so sis. I am sorry. Are you ok?" Bianca asked.

"I am pissed right now." I said.

"I would be too." Bianca said.

"Where is he at?" Nikita asked.

"At home and I am heading back there right now."

"I'm coming wit'chu." Nikita said.

There I was. Due any day, and pissed because I'd found out what I already knew. That my man was cheating on me. If I wasn't ignoring the obvious red flags again, I would have known sooner. I didn't know if he was having unprotected sex with that nasty looking, rat ass bitch either. I know I was having sex with him unprotected, so he could have easily exposed me and my baby to something. I was taking short breaths as I was making back to back calls to Wesley's phone. Nikita was driving, and I was so angry I felt like I would hyperventilate. Wes not answering his phone made me angrier. I felt anxious to get home, so I could confront him.

When we got there, I waddled my big ass in the house and popped Wes upside his head. Nikita was standing right behind me waiting for his ass to do something. Nikita had a gun in her purse and was not afraid to use it.

"Who is this bitch coming to my shop talking about you are her man!?" I yelled

"What!? I don't know who you are talking about!" he yelled.

"You know who I'm talking about! Lesley is her name!"

"Hell nah! That's one of cuz's homegirls! I ain't fucking with that bitch!"

"You're lying Wes!"

"I'm not!"

"So why would she come to my shop! I'm so sick of your shit! I'm thirty-eight weeks pregnant and I'm finding out that you are cheating on me with a ratchet ass bitch like that!?"

I broke down. I started crying uncontrollably. When people say the straw that broke the camel's back. That was the straw that broke me. Nikita held me in her arms while I cried.

"Baby no. please don't cry." Wes said. He tried to touch me, but I yelled, "Get out Wes!"

"Baby."

"GET OUT!"

"I think that you should go." Nikita said to him.

Wes grabbed some of his things and left. Nikita stayed with me. She had Jakari drop their son off at my house so she could stay by my side. She was worried about me. I was close to my due date, and she knew how Wesley was after drinking because of the last time I kicked him out.

Lesley was the second chick that came to my shop about Wes. Another surprise secret about Wes. I was truly numb. All that, and then my water broke that night. I woke up around two o'clock in the morning. I felt like I was peeing on myself, then, I realized what had happened. I was too pissed at Wes, but I called him anyways to let him know that I was on my way to the hospital. I didn't want to hear his voice or see his face, but he was the father so it was only right that he knew. He showed up at the hospital right away smelling like alcohol and weed. I was in too much pain to even care.

Then, I cried, I moaned, I groaned, I tossed, I turned, I screamed, I cursed the day that I got pregnant, and when I thought I couldn't take it anymore, I did it. I gave birth to the most beautiful angel that I had ever seen and it was over. I couldn't believe that something so beautiful could be born in the middle of the hell that I was living in, but she made it. All ten fingers, and ten toes. Beautiful brown eyes, and full lips like her father. My mom and Nikita cried. Wes even shed a tear when he held her for the first time.

I was so in love with my little girl, I couldn't even think about what happened at my shop the day before. Wes was in love too; he barley wanted to stop holding her. After all our family and friends showed up to the hospital to shower us with love and gifts, we took our baby girl home.

I paid Wes no mind when we got back home. I gave him the cold shoulder for the first couple of weeks. All my attention was on my brand-new baby. All of Wes's attention was on her too. The house was peaceful, and Wes did not leave one time.

I guess Wes grew tired of me not talking to him, and us not addressing the elephant in the room. He decided to approach me. I had just finished putting Ava back into her bassinet and sat down on the couch with a fashion magazine in my hand. It was the magazine that Chanel works for. I had just gotten the newest monthly publication in the mail and I was excited to see what was going to be popular in fashion for the fall. I had also gotten the new Black Hair magazine in the mail. I planned to read through that after I finished the fashion magazine. I always loved to stay up to date with beauty and fashion.

"Can we talk?" Wes asked. He was sitting in the lazy boy chair with the television remote in his hand.

"If you're ready to tell the truth." I said without looking up from the magazine.

"I am."

"Ok. I'm listening." I said.

"Can you look at me" I took a deep breath, closed the magazine, and set it on the coffee table. I turned my full body towards Wes.

"You can't turn up though Adara."

"Wesley talk."

He sighed and said, "When you kicked me out, me and Lesley got cool hanging over at my cousin's. I started going to her house to smoke n shit." he paused.

"And?"

"I fucked her once, and I hate that I did it. I told her that I couldn't mess with her like that anymore and she got to tripping."

I could feel tears start to burn my eyes. "You fucked her?" I asked.

"One time bae."

"Don't tell me no half ass lie Wesley."

"I'm not bae. I am telling you the truth. I fucked her one time and I shouldn't have done that."

"And she was giving you money, right?"

"She helped me out from time to time."

"Damn Wesley! How could you!?" I dabbed a few tears the had fallen from my eyes.

"I'm sorry baby. I wasn't thinking. I will never do it again I promise." I just want to fix what I have with you so I can be here for my daughter." He stood up and walked over to sit on the couch next to me.

"Do you know how stupid you made me look arguing with that chick in front of my shop! I've been through hell and back with you because of your job situation and your drinking problem, but you go and cheat on me too!" I said. I couldn't stop my tears. I let them soak my face.

"Baby I know that I have been a fuck up. Please forgive me. I can make this right. I can make this all go away."

"You say that every time Wesley. How? How are you gonna make it right?"

"I'm done drinking, I am going to find a real job. I will never do no shit like that again. I missed out on my youngest son growing up because I was locked up. I don't want to miss out on my daughter over some stupid shit."

I shook my head, folded my arms across my chest, and rolled my eyes. He had the nerve to let tears fall from his eyes. I couldn't feel any sympathy for him. I was so disgusted by him. I couldn't believe he had the nerve to cheat on me. I had been with him for three years and had turned down many offers for his raggedy ass.

"Baby please give me another chance. Please." he said as he scooted closer to me on the couch.

"Move Wes. The baby is crying." I stood up and walked towards our baby's room.

Chapter 21

My mom planned a welcome party for my baby Ava. She likes doing welcome parties over baby showers because people can meet the baby. It's still a baby shower to me. It's just done after the baby is born. I always thought her way of doing it was weird because I was used to the traditional way, but over the years I had gotten used to it. She threw a couple of welcome parties for my brother's kids, and a couple for my cousins.

All my family and friends were in attendance. Everyone went all out with the gifts they bought for my first-born baby girl. Wes's mom, dad, and brother flew in for the party. Wes was there and to my surprise he was not drunk. My mother out did herself on the food and decorations. We had the celebration in a large banquet hall on the first floor of a hotel. It worked out perfect for Wes's family. They rented rooms in that same hotel for the weekend.

Wes and I were all smiles in front of the family. We were putting on a show. The truth was, we still weren't talking at home. I wasn't happy and I was not feeling Wes at all. Thoughts of him messing with Lesley consumed my mind and made me sick to my stomach daily. To make matters worse, the chick had started harassing me. She had been calling and texting my phone non- stop. I started to block her, but I decided to keep the records for evidence in case I decided to press charges on her. She was even calling the shop making threats. I admit that she had me feeling like telling her where she could come and meet me. Nikita was down too.

"I'ma beat her ass on sight cousin." Nikita told me.

There I was, a grown woman, thinking about putting my hands on some chick my man cheated on me with. Then, she started sending me text messages of conversations that she had with Wes. All the way up to the night that I gave birth to Ava. He was expressing his love and wanting to be with her, and there were some explicit texts. Things about him wanting to bend her over and dick her down. Obviously, she was sending me everything that Wes had conveniently erased from his phone. Those texts messages showed me that they were together more than the one time that he claimed to have slept with her.

He had apologized a million times, but I wasn't interested in hearing it. We weren't talking at all at home. It was worse than when we brought Ava home from the hospital. We were sleeping separately. I slept in my office that I converted into Ava's room. He slept in our room or on the couch.

After I finished breast feeding Ava, I handed her to one of my aunts. She couldn't wait to hold baby Ava. I walked over to my mom to help her straighten up and cut the cake.

"Girl go sit down." My mom said to me when I walked up.

"I want to help." I said.

"Alright well cover up that macaroni and cheese for me please." she said, then, she two stepped a little to the R

Kelly song that was playing through the loud speakers. She sang a few of the lyrics to "Step in The Name of Love," along with the song. She grabbed my hand and made me step with her a little bit before I walked over to the table where most of the food was.

I pulled the aluminum foil down over the pan of baked macaroni and cheese. I smiled at my mom. She was working a one-piece halter jump suit with wide leg. The material clung to her body showing off her tight figure. My mom always has it going on. I felt jealous of her body. My body didn't bounce back like some of the women I knew that had babies. My stomach still felt flabby, I had gotten some stretch marks, and my breasts were still huge.

I looked across the room and saw Wes heading outside with his brother. That meant they were going to smoke and have brother talk. They might even slip a drink in. The thought of them slipping in a drink made me a little worried, but I trusted that he would not take that risk with all our family there.

Looking at Wes made me think about how much I hated that his trifling ass was still at my house. I wanted to tell him to get out like I had done several times before, but my heart wouldn't let me pull him away from his daughter.

Wes was so happy with her. I could see love in his eyes when he looked at her. He was so in love with Ava. I hadn't seen Wes like that since we first met. I knew that I was being stupid again, but I was giving him a chance to be a father to his child.

Wes was home every day with me and Ava. He hadn't been drinking or hanging out with his cousin Quinten. Every time Ava cried in the middle of the night, he would jump up to come into the room to see what was wrong and help. Although my love for him wasn't there, I loved seeing him with his daughter. Wes was putting his best foot forward, but my anger and disappointment would not allow me to forgive him for what he did. Plus, I was still being harassed by Lesley every day. He'd even tried checking Lesley to prove to me that he was done with her, but she wasn't having it. Lesley was extremely angry that he was home with me, and she was going to do everything in her power to sabotage what she assumed he had with me. Part of me understood after I saw the text messages, but I wasn't with all the disrespect and the threats.

"What are you gonna do about Wes?" My mom asked me in a low voice. She made sure no one could hear her over the music. She removed the cover from the cake, and began cutting it into small squares. My mom and I are close, so I told her about what was going on with Wes. She was disappointed to say the least.

'I don't know mom. I love him and I am trying to make this work for Ava. I want him to be in his daughter's life, but I don't know if it's worth it."

"Um hum." she said. "Hand me those plates over there." She pointed to the other table with all the utensils. I handed her the small pink plates. The plates matched all the pink decorations in the room.

"How has he been doing with that drinking?" she asked.

"He hasn't been drinking for the last couple months."

"That's good. Job?"

"I have been helping him look for one."

"Again Adara?"

"Yes. He isn't internet savvy."

"But I bet he knows how to navigate Facebook and Instagram." she said. She had a point. I knew Wes could learn how to do it on his own. I just didn't feel like dealing with his attitude whenever I tried to teach him, so I did it for him.

"You know I want the best for my first grandbaby, but I went through the same stuff with your father. He could never seem to get himself together. I just don't want to see you go through that same thing, and waste years of your life trying to fix someone who is broken. Who doesn't want to fix themselves." I nodded my head. We saw Wes come back in, so we shut down the conversation and began setting the plates of cake slices out on the empty table.

Chapter 22

I was back to work at the shop after being home for three months. Three months off work seems like a blessing, but it drove me crazy. I was bored with my life and sick of seeing Wes every day, all day. Daytime television had run its course. I was up to date on all the celebrity gossip, and all the crime and issues in the world. I had binge watched all the popular television series. I think Power, Queen Sugar, and Orange Is the New Black, were my favorite ones. I had organized everything in my house. I'd even color coordinated my closet. I did a bunch of spring cleaning and threw a bunch of things out. I donated my gently used clothes to the homeless shelter. Then, I ran out of things to do, and I was over being at home.

I was worried about putting Ava into day care too soon, so my mom agreed to baby sit Ava while I was at work. I decided to be at the shop part time, so I could be home with Ava more. It worked out perfectly, and I was back to making money again. Being at home had also set me back financially again, so I was eager to get all my clients back into my chair. I needed to get my income back to the way that it was before Wes and Ava. I was working hard every day. I was even taking my VIP clients on Sunday's and Monday's when the shop was closed.

Bianca had done a great job at keeping the shop together, and collecting the booth rent from the stylists while I was gone. She'd even taken on a few of my clients in my absence. I couldn't have picked a better person to hold down the fort. I made plans to take her out and treat her to dinner. I invited Nikita and Chanel to come along since I hadn't seen either one of them in a while. I was ecstatic when my mom said that she would keep Ava for me, so I could go out with my girls and have some girls time. I had been home with my baby for six months and I needed some time for me. All of us met up at a restaurant downtown Minneapolis.

They squealed when I walked in. I was slowly getting my body back to the way it was, but it was a work in progress.

"Look at you girl!" Chanel said.

"Yea your looking good cousin!" Nikita said.

"Thanks ladies! I am trying to get my sexy back." I said as I sat down next to Chanel.

Bianca said, "I told you that you would sis."

"Thanks sis." I said to her.

After we ordered drinks, Chanel looked at me and said, "I've got something to show you."

"What?" I asked.

She pulled off her red, Ralph Lauren, leather gloves that she was wearing, and revealed a huge, sparkling, engagement ring.

"I'm getting married!" she exclaimed with a big smile.

"Oh wow! I was wondering why you were wearing those hot ass leather gloves in the summer time. I thought it was some bougie shit." Nikita said.

"Shut up." she said to Nikita.

"Congratulations sis." I said. I wasn't as enthusiastic as I should have been. My unhappiness with my life didn't allow me to feel cheerful with her exciting news.

"The ring is gorgeous sis. Who is he? The guy that you didn't want to tell me about the last time you were here?" I asked as I held her hand up so I could get a closer look of the ring. It was beautiful and Chanel was glowing. I had never seen her look so happy.

"Let me see girl!" Nikita took Chanel's hand to look at the ring.

"Girl this is nice! He must have money." Nikita said.

"He does. He makes seven figures."

"Damn! What does he do?" Nikita asked.

I was surprised that Nikita and Chanel were having a civilized conversation without bickering.

"He is a professional athlete. He is an NFL player. Don't give me that look Adara. He is a good guy."

"You got a baller girl. Good for you and congratulations." Bianca said. She had been quiet that day which was not like her. I knew that she was going through some things with her boo, so I figured that was the reason.

"I am happy for you sis." I said.

"I would like for you to be my maid of honor." Chanel said to me.

"Anything for you sister." I said and reached over to hug her.

"Awww." Bianca said.

"Nikita, I would like for you to be one of my bridesmaids and before you say anything, I am paying for everything. I will be paying for your dresses, your hair and make-up, and your trip to New York."

"Wow Chanel. I am down!" Nikita said excitedly.

"Why aren't you having the wedding here at home?" I asked with an attitude.

"Because we want to have it at his fabulous house in New York."

"You could have had it at a church here." I said with more attitude.

"His house is amazing sis. Just wait, you will see."

I admit, I was being petty. My energy was off and I could feel Nikita and Bianca looking at me.

I said, "I am sure that it will be beautiful wherever it is sis. I can't wait. Congratulations." I leaned over and kissed her on the cheek. "Excuse me for a minute." I said to everyone.

I stood up and walked to the bathroom. I closed and locked the door and walked over to the mirror. I looked at my reflection. I was stressed. I had covered up the heavy bags under my eyes with some make-up I had gotten from Sephora. I wasn't happy in my relationship with Wes. I was back to smoking cigarettes again and I had started drinking more. Mostly wine, but it was on an everyday basis. I never drank to get drunk, but I did it to feel a buzz, or to relax so I could go to sleep. I never thought that taking care of a baby, working, and dealing with an alcoholic would be so much work. I was mentally, emotionally, and physically drained.

Wes was drinking again. It started when he went back to work. He made a couple of friends who liked to go out and have beers after work. They weren't aware of his situation, and didn't know that they were pulling him back into a habit that he was trying hard to stay away from. Wes was weak and he gave in to temptation. He started coming home with the smell of beer on his breath. When I questioned him about it he would say that is was only beer.

"It's still alcohol and you know that you have a drinking problem." I would tell him.

"I am not an alcoholic Adara. Chill out." He would say back to me, and round and round we would go about if he was an alcoholic or not. He knew and I knew the truth, and we both knew that with alcohol came the other things like his uncontrollable emotions. Particularly, his temper was his main problem. I wasn't trying to deal with that crap; not with Ava in the house.

I told him that I felt he should seek some professional help for his problem. He told me that he wasn't trying to hear it. I had been thinking long and hard about ending it with Wes permanently. For a while we weren't talking at all at home, but over time the silence went away and we began talking again. The next thing I knew, we were making love again, and I was back into a full-blown relationship with Wes.

I was trying to hold it together for Ava, but the truth was, I wasn't happy and I hadn't been for a long time. I had been through too much with Wes and I had reached the end of my rope with the whole thing. Three-years had gone by and my primary thought about Wes and I was, "I'm done." I was done with the drama, the lies, the skeleton's, the bullshit, the drinking, the income issues. I was tired of being broke, and hustling my ass off to make ends meet every time he was unemployed.

Our four-year anniversary was slowly approaching and we had gotten nowhere in our relationship. I didn't even know why I was still wearing his engagement ring.

I looked down at my ring. I took it off my finger, held it in my hand, and I began to cry.

Chapter 23

"Hol'up baby don't move. I don't want to cum yet."
Wes whispered in my ear. His head was rested on my
shoulder while he laid on top of me. He was trying to catch
his bearings. I rolled my eyes up to the ceiling. I swore his
freak came out when he was drunk off some Hennessy. He
would want to be in me all night, and I wasn't feeling it. I
was hoping that it would be a quickie. I should have known
better when I watched him take his third shot of Hennessy.

He kissed my shoulder, my neck, and then my lips.
He stuck his tongue into my mouth. I could taste

Hennessey on his tongue as he gave me a passionate tongue kiss that I didn't want. He began to pump in and out of me again at a slow motion until he felt like he had control. Then, he started pounding more aggressively. He put my legs over his shoulders and plunged even deeper into me. Usually I would be screaming when he did that, but I wasn't there mentally. The sound of my headboard hitting the wall was more entertaining than him. I wasn't feeling it. At that moment, I knew that I had checked out of the relationship with Wes.

I honestly wanted to lay there like a dead fish until he got his, but since it was our four- year anniversary I decided to participate a little bit. He did take me out to dinner and a movie, so I mustered up some energy to moan a little for him. I also figured it would help him hurry up and cum, so he could get off me. I was trying to make him cum quick before he stopped me the first time. I wanted to get it over with, but he was steadily trying to make love to me.

Ugh would you hurry up and cum so I can go to bed. I thought. Ava would be up in the morning, and I would be the one to get up with her. She was nine-months and she was sleeping through the night finally. Wes slept all morning before he had to go to work, so I would be up feeding, changing diapers, and chasing her around the house.

"Damn this pussy good baby." He moaned in my ear. I kept my eyes on the ceiling. He was finally about to come. Before he pulled out, he told me that he loved me. Once he laid down next to me, I got out of bed and went straight to the bathroom to take a shower.

"Bae where are you going?" Wes asked.

"To take a shower." I said.

"You couldn't lay with me for a second?"

"Yes, after I get cleaned up. I am sweaty Wes." I said with little emotion. I looked at my engagement ring again. I was trying to hold us together for our baby, but I couldn't take it anymore. I was still trying to dig myself out of a financial hole because of him. I was barely holding on to my house, my car, and my business at that point. The little that he was bringing in from his temporary job was helping a little, but the job assignment was about to end. I wasn't sure if I wanted him in my house when it did. I would be digging myself an even deeper hole if he was. Especially if he didn't get put on another job right away.

Plus, he was coming home late and drunk again. Some nights he would be talking crazy to me. Other nights he would wake Ava up because he was loud, then, he would pass out and leave me to deal with her.

I felt a strong urge to go back into our bedroom and tell him that I was done. I didn't want all the ruckus he would cause if I did that, so I just closed my eyes and allowed the hot shower water to ease my stress. A few minutes later, I heard the bathroom door open. Wes came into the bathroom and got in with me. He was trying so hard to be romantic with me, but I couldn't get into it. *I should have locked the door.* I thought.

"You know I love you, right?" he said to me. It took everything in me not to roll my eyes at him.

"Really Wes?" I asked sarcastically.

"Really Adara? Your questioning my love?"

"I am questioning why you do the things that you do?"

He sighed, "What are you talking about bae? I ain't doing nothing but going to work and coming home to my girls."

"Are you sure?"

"Bae stop. Why are you trying to ruin this night with your questions? Yes, bae I am sure. I love you. I ain't got nothing else going on."

"Ok, but you're drinking a lot again."

"No I am not. I was drinking with you tonight. Are you gonna put every little thing I do underneath a magnifying glass?"

"That is not what I am doing. Tonight, is not the only night that you have been drinking."

"Look, can I at least wash your body babe?"

"No I am getting out."

"Aw that's cold Adara. Are we still going out tomorrow?"

"Yes."

"Aight cool. I bought you something that I would like for you to wear."

"What?" I asked while drying off.

"You'll see."

***

Although I wasn't feeling Wes, it did feel good to be out. I hadn't been out and feeling sexy in a long time. If I wasn't at home changing poopy diapers, I was at the shop standing on my feet for hours. He surprised me with tickets to a Tank concert, and an outfit to wear to the concert. The dress fit perfectly. I had finally gotten my body back to the way I like it, so I was feeling myself. I was having a great time with Wes. We danced and we laughed, and he wasn't drinking. I guess because I had mentioned it the night before. I was happy that he decided to be on his best behavior. It felt like old times, and I could see why I fell in love with him.

"Excuse me! What the fuck are you doing here with this bitch Wesley!" I heard Lesley's squeaky voice yell from behind us. Wes and I were walking through the parking lot to our car. Both of us turned around.

"Hello!?" she yelled.

"Lesley go on with that bullshit." Wes said.

"Did you tell that bitch that you were with me the other night Wes!?"

"That bitch is standing right here! You can address me by my name if you have something to say to me!" I yelled.

"Shut the fuck up bitch!" she yelled.

"No, you shut the fuck up!" I yelled.

"Lesley chill out!" Wes yelled at her.

"Fuck no Wes! You told me that you were done with her!" she yelled at him.

"Well you can see that he's not." I said and flashed my engagement ring.

POW.

The bitch swung and hit me right in my head. "Bitch!" I yelled. I started swinging. She punched me a couple of times and I punch her a couple of times and then I got a hold of her hair. I kept punching her in her head. She kept swinging on me but she wasn't landing anymore punches. I was dragging her around that parking lot by her hair. People started crowding around, watching and recording the fight. All I was thinking about was killing that bitch. I didn't think about the fact that I could possibly be on YouTube, Hood Fights, or World Star. That bitch was gonna know not to ever fuck with me again. I had her hair in one hand and I kept punching her with the other. She was struggling to try to get up off the ground and pry my hands from her hair. I could hear Wes and some other people trying to break it up. I didn't know how long I was fighting. I had blacked out. That bitch was gonna pay for all the bullshit that she had been talking. I was handling her like I was one of the WWE Divas. Wes was finally able to pull me away from her. I kicked her in the chest when he pulled me away from her.

"Bitch I told you I would drag your ass!" I yelled. I had blood dripping from my lip. I spit it on the ground. Somebody was holding her. I wasn't sure if they were people that she knew, or people from the audience that we drew around us. Wes damn near carried me to the car, forced me inside, and pulled off. All the while, I was still yelling across the parking lot about how Lesley had me fucked up. My adrenaline was pumping and I could feel my heart was beating hard and extremely fast. I started yelling at Wes.

"You got me fucked up Wesley! You're still fucking that bitch!" I started to cry. "You got me fighting bitches over you! Look at my lip!" I looked down at my nails and two were broken. One of them was broken down to the skin. It was bleeding and my finger was throbbing.

"Look at my fucking nails!"

"Bae I'm sorry! She was lying! I don't know what was wrong with that bitch babe!"

"I have never had to fight a female over a guy and you got bitches attacking me!" I pulled down the visor mirror to look at my lip.

"Look at this shit! Wes!"

"Bae calm down! That chick was out of pocket!"

"Fuck calming down! You're still cheating on me Wesley! I'm done! I don't want to do this anymore!"

"Bae!"

"I don't want to hear shit!"

We pulled up to my mom's house so we could pick up Ava.

"I'm done! I'm staying here!" I said when he parked in front of my mom's house. I jumped out of his car. He jumped out of his car too and darted over to me. He grabbed me to hold me to stop me from walking, but I pushed him off me and started swinging at him. "Get away from me Wesley!"

He was blocking my punches with his arms and trying to grab me at the same time. I whopped him upside his head a couple of times. "Adara Stop!" he yelled. He grabbed both of my arms and pulled me to him to restrain me. My back was up again his chest and he had my arms folded in front of me. "Baby stop. Ok. Stop. Please. I love you. calm down." he said into my ear. Both of us were out of breath.

"I've been calm. I've been calm for too long Wes. It's all my fault because I keep letting you do this to me. I'm done. I'm staying here."

"Adara listen baby, you are tripping right now. Let's go home and talk about this."

"I am done talking about this! I'm done! You have to go!" I yelled and started struggling to get away from him.

"Stop Adara! I ain't going nowhere!"

"Yes, you are!"

My mom heard us and came to the door. "What's going on out here? It's late."

I stopped moving.

"We are alright mom; I am about to come in." I said. "Let me go Wes." He released me and stepped back.

"I don't know what is going on, but you are making too much noise out here."

"Here I come mom."

I turned to him and said, "Be gone when I get home. Get all of your shit and get out." He had tears in his eyes. He looked like he wanted to say more, or put up a fight, but he didn't.

"I'm sorry Ms. Lewis." He said and walked back to his car, got in, and pulled off.

"What happened to you? I know that he didn't put his hands on you." My mom said with a look of concern on her face.

"No mom. I got into a fight with a chick at the concert." I said as I walked into her house.

"Oh, my goodness, girl you know you are too cute to be fighting."

I shook my head. I did know that I was too cute to be fighting over some raggedy ass dude. I was still stunned by the whole ordeal. I told my mom all about what happened. Once I was done explaining the whole thing, I said, "I'm done mom. I can't do it anymore."

I meant it that time. I spent the night at my mom's. She drove me home the next day. Wes was gone. He took all his stuff as I asked, and he left peacefully. I'm glad he did because I just didn't have it in me to deal with anything else. My mom and I walked through the house to make sure everything was alright before we put Ava down onto her feet. As I walked through my house, I realized how relieved I was to see my closets clean and free of Wes's things. At that moment, I knew that I was done. I was tired, I was down to my last, and my patience was gone. I had given everything I had until I had nothing left to give. Wes was a fuck boy, and I was the woman who loved him. I put up with Wes because I love him, but I couldn't deal with it anymore. That fight with Lesley put the nail in the coffin for him. I loved Wes with all my heart and soul. All I wanted, was for Wesley to do right, so we could be together forever. In the process, I allowed Wes to almost ruin my life. I put all my focus into Wesley, and lost sight of Adara. It was time to get my life back and let my fuck boy go.

A month later:

Wesley: Adara, I know that you hate me. I would hate me too. I should have done better. I could have treated you better, but I didn't. I made a lot of mistakes I know that can't be erased. I admit, I was lazy about getting and keeping a job. I let my drinking get the best of me, and I apologize bae. I need you baby. I ain't right without you. I miss you and my daughter. I pray every day that you will forgive me, and give me another chance.

Adara: I'm Good.

I was, and I had never felt better.

Acknowledgements

Shout out to my family. I appreciate you guys for having my back through the tough times. I love you! Shout out to my friends who remain patient with me when I don't respond to calls or texts because I am too busy writing or editing my book projects. Thank you! Shout out to all my readers! I appreciate you for giving me a chance. Shout out to all the authors out there who are following their dreams! Don't give up. Keep pushing and doing what you love. Shout out to anyone I forgot. To all the women who have ever dealt with a fuck boy. Mama you don't have to go through that. You deserve better. Keep telling yourself that. There is someone out there who will love you the way that you deserve to be loved. To everyone, always remember to live, laugh, and love. Smooches!

-Nia Rich

CPSIA information can be obtained
at www.ICGtesting.com
Printed in the USA
BVHW040216241120
594094BV00027B/456